The Family

Brother and Sister Love

Calvin L Himel

The Family

All Rights Reserved

Copyright. 2020
ISBN: 978-1-0878-6103-6
EPUB: 978-0-5786-3669-6
First printing: January, 2020

Cover Design by: Lemih

Introduction

This is a love story, unlike any other, but probably one that has more than likely occurred, somewhere on our planet many times throughout world history. I thought it to be an interesting subject since love is like a bird making a nest. In my own person   al life it has also come and gone, through various and differing circumstances, such as divorce and death. It is a very wonderful and fulfilling feeling when you really find it and the true happiness it brings.

I again would like to thank my very dear wife who is the reason why I have started this particular endeavor and all by accident after retiring. When she told me that I needed to find something to do with my time, well this is that something along with a skill I didn't think I possessed fully even though my mother had shown me what to do when I was a young child, and that was sewing. I continue to look for more endeavors along with building my own computers and playing interactive video games. We live in such a wonderful time, and one in which we bear such a heavy responsibility to guide the world forward on the right path of self-preservation for the planet an all humanity.

All I wish for is that you enjoy this story and maybe even the others I have written. I wish all my readers well, and hope everyone has a fulfilling and joyful life.

Thank You. Calvin L Himel
October 2019

The Family

Chapter One

The large beautiful art deco apartment building stood as an example of the most advanced, futuristic and most advanced thinking in architecture at the time of its construction when it was built during the nineteen twenties. It was steel frame and concrete and one of the first buildings to ever be built with a fire suppression system throughout the entire building and had retained all of its beautiful art deco interior and exterior features because the building had remained in the possession of the family that had built it. They lived here and had always resided within its sturdy walls and maintained it with loving care over the many decades. It wasn't your average run of the mill apartment buildings, it had a very special charm and the craftsmanship throughout was superb and the best money could buy, then and even now. The apartments were beyond exceptional, every one being very large, spacious and comfortable. The owners had constantly kept updating the building by rehabbing it completely several times over the decades as technology progressed and most recently just a couple of years ago. The sprinkler system had been updated in all of the units and throughout the entire building several times over the years and a complete system was added to the adjoining parking garage. It was built at the same time as the apartment building but didn't have a fire suppression system installed when it was built, but now had the newest and the most advanced CO_2 suppression system available. The new system had been added a year ago now and was fully operational. It was luxury apartments with a charm like you wouldn't find anywhere else in the entire busy metropolis where it was located. The buildings footprint was half a block square with streets on three sides and if you included the garage, it would be an entire city block. There were some single story exclusive stores located in the garage building on the lower level, mostly salons and exclusive boutiques.

There were only eight apartments per floor from the third to the tenth floor, then six per floor, from eleven to the twentieth floor, then four per floor, from twenty-first to the thirty forth, until you came to the thirty-fifth floor and then there were only two, they both were extremely large duplex penthouse apartments. The average number of bed rooms were three below ten, then four up to twentieth floor, then six bed rooms with each having their own large private baths up to the thirty-fifth floor, Each apartment had a dining room, a large living room, a library not to mention a kitchen with a pantry, and each bed room had its own bathroom. There also was two large freight or service elevators in the rear next to the wide rear stairway. There was a bank of twelve beautiful elevators which gave it a feeling of true exclusivity, and the penthouse apartments had their own private elevator. The décor was special with a lot of charm and had a very warm feel everywhere you looked, something not found in many of the modern architecture masterpieces of today. All the units had marvelous expansive views of the broad park across the street because of the exceptionally large windows which when the building was built were cutting edge. It was a block wide and half a block square and had views on all four of its sides with the exception of the rear units that bordered the adjoining garage below the eight floors. There the rear windows facing the garage and all had frosted glass to add to the privacy and there was also a large open space between the two buildings. You can imagine that the rents were expensive by everyday standards, but there had always been a long waiting list for any vacancies since the address was one of the most prestigious in the city if not the most prestigious among all of the rental apartment buildings. It was thirty-six stories tall with the first floor lobby being two stories tall and very open with a beautiful lobby like a luxury hotel with a cocktail lounge on the ground floor and having a beautiful and very expansive mezzanine where the building management office was located along with a laundry, dry cleaners, barber shop and two exclusive hair salons and a beautiful waiting area adding to the large, beautiful lobby with its bank of elevators. The buildings unseen space was where the trash was deposited in the rear by the garage, which was collected and deposited via a large garbage chute from all the floors above, on a daily basis. Rents ran an average of $20,000.00 per month for the apartments located on the lower floors, and increased as you progressed upwards, because of the location and amenities. There was even a fitness center on the ground floor for residents only, with a steam room, with an Olympic size swimming pool that was all part of the original design. Residents could have a massage, pedicure and several other special personal services performed. The lobby was cleaned twice daily as you would expect as was the fitness center. The exterior facade was exceptionally maintained and included a door

man, twenty four hours a day. The thirty-fifth floor had
only two units and both were duplex apartments with a
terrace on the thirty-sixth floor and additional bedrooms
that almost doubled the size of the two extremely large
apartments. The owner's son and daughter Mr. Roger
Oliver White resided in 35A along with his sister Ms.
Susan Anne Stone. His father and mother, Mr. George
Roger Harrison White and Mrs. Ethel Anne Stone White
resided in 35B. Mr. George Harrisons grandfather had
built the building when quality materials were very
inexpensive and labor and superb craftsmanship were
even more so, and had grown up in the building himself.
Roger and Susan's parents had married after both had
spouses who had passed away just a couple years apart,
and when they both were in their early pre-teen years.
Roger was nine and Susan was ten when their parents
married. The children got along exceptionally well with
one another considering they had only met one another
only once or twice before their parents' marriage. They
quickly developed a deep and very close personal
relationship with one another and especially after they
began living in the same household which was very rare
for most stepchildren. As a matter of fact they really
loved one another and this love would continue to
flourish and grow stronger through the coming years
especially as they matured and entered into adulthood to
become more than just you're average run of the mill
brother and sister relationship.

Both siblings loved both of their parents very much,
and obeyed their strict parental rules as they grew up
together, very seldom ever giving their parents any

reason to reprimand or punish them. They kept each other out of trouble and really stuck together. Roger gradually grew closer to his stepmother Ethel over time, she had such a caring nature as did Susan to George her stepfather and they lived in a very happy and most loving house hold. Both children had attended the prestigious St. Georges Academy for there early school years, and then the adjoining and very exclusive high school, the St. George Thomas Academy School of Science. Susan graduated number three in the top five of her class and a year before Roger who was number five in the top ten in his class. The following year after he graduated and working a summer job, he took some advanced math and business classes at the nearby local junior college as Roger dreamed of starting his own company one day. Both went on to attend the same prestigious university, both also had graduated from law school, getting their law degrees and eventually their license. Roger also had a degree in business and Susan one in finance. They had been taught from an early age that they would someday take over the reins of the family business; the White Company which was a highly respected and successful family owned Investment Company with a large portfolio of assets and controlled a vast assortment of stocks, bonds, and real estate investments, and several other lucrative family business endeavors. Even though they were well to do and their parents had paid for their education, both had to work to support their own personal expenses while they attended college. Both had several jobs while attending university and did quite well for themselves. Roger ended up buying the apartment building he lived in while attending college by his second year instead of buying a car and by the time he had graduated, owned three more apartment buildings which he eventually over time rehabbed and rented out at slightly higher rents than before he purchased them. Roger worked several jobs during his time at college, at a gas station, book store, a restaurant waiting tables and finely at a real estate office where he soon acquired his broker's license which he wouldn't need after he passed the bar exam. He did quite well for himself and Susan during his four and a half years in college.

Susan worked in a restaurant and a strip club for a very short time and finally a department store. The strip club job didn't last long, just about a week because she was afraid of what her parents might think, but especially after Roger found out and said he didn't want her working there and said he would provide for her before he would let her demean herself. That is when Susan knew Roger really and truly loved her and she loved him even more as he provided for her financial needs. Susan and Roger attended the same university and shared an apartment together during their years at school together. When Roger bought his first building with the tuition money for his sophomore year, he was soon paying his tuition back after collecting rents. His father never knew what he had done and it was a big gamble Roger had taken. Both Roger and Susan dated other people off and on, but their relationships with others didn't ever last long, or more than a couple weeks and all outside relationships came to an abrupt end upon graduation for both. Roger was a very handsome young man, six foot tall, slim; with a beautiful olive completion, brunet hair and Susan was five foot ten, light olive completion, slim, very shapely, long dark brown hair, with a beautiful face and keen features. You would never know they were brother and sister when they stood side by side.

Upon graduation with Susan being the first to finish college, she began working at The White Company as an intern, and soon worked her way to becoming a junior manager in the real-estate and investment department after two years. After Roger joined the company it didn't take him long either after he passed the bar exam along with Susan to advance. An in the two years after joining the company he became the number ten person in the legal department out of fourteen who worked there, and not because of who he was, but because he was that sharp. There were only about thirty five employees total at the White Company.

They were both enjoying a wonderful life and Roger was the recipient of a trust fund his grandmother had left him in her will and she had also provided some money for Susan before she passed on. Roger took and used the sixty seven million dollars to buy his first hi-rise residential apartment building, after rehabbing it moved in with Susan and it wasn't long before he bought another building after the developer began having serious financial problems and trouble completing the project. Roger used his building as collateral and with Susan's financial help took over the project and completed its construction. That's when he and Susan moved into the penthouse at the ultra-modern and newly constructed Sutton Place. This was the beginning of his and Susan's

soon to be vast real estate and Restaurant Empire. They
had no idea at the time about the direction they together
were headed as Susan contemplated opening a night club.
Before they knew it he was preparing to purchase an
entire city block of several large century old industrial
buildings way before the neighborhood was beginning to
show signs of becoming gentrified and purchased the
properties relatively cheap compared to several years
later as they appreciated in value. He immediately began
to rehab and refurbishes every building turning them into
beautiful state of the art facilities up to date facilities and
soon was able to turn them into the place to be. He
quickly acquired several more nearby buildings and soon
owned the majority of the properties for several square
blocks and became the driving force behind gentrification
in the area with his soon to be vast holdings, and was
able to benefit greatly from his investments. It's how and
where Susan eventually opened her first night club, and
soon in the same blocks her first restaurant and bar. That
was the beginning, when she opened, Whips and Chains,
it was her entry into the night club and restaurant
business and soon after she opened the second restaurant
in another portion of the same block long property that
Roger owned. They began investing more of their money
back into each of their endeavors. Roger had just about
replenished all the cash from his and Susan's trust funds.

When the extremely long term tenant of 35B passed
away after thirty three years, and five years after Roger
had graduated college and his heirs moved and disposed
of all his personal possessions, and decided to terminate
the lease agreement on the apartment. Mr. White offered

the unit to Roger, who accepted it right away and then had the entire apartment refurbished from the floor, to the ceiling. Roger always loved living there as a boy and it was a no brainer when his father offered him the adjoining penthouse unit. Roger informally moved in nine months later after all the work had been completed, mostly updating the bathrooms and kitchen, making them even more modern. And since he owned the building he lived in prior to moving back home he was in no particular rush. He occupied the very top floor, the penthouse and he offered it to his sister. Susan had her own apartment in the same building; rent free just below his and when Roger told her about the apartment next to their parents he offered her a bedroom. Susan said she would rather live with him after several breakups with various men, for different reasons. She told Roger about all the men she met and it seemed all they wanted was her financial support and weren't any good in bed anyway. Roger told her they would always have each other and didn't need anyone else. That's when she let her apartment go and they decided they didn't need anyone else in their love life and would live together and have each other in an exclusive relationship.

Their love affair first became sexual when they were just entering adolescence. It started when Susan accidentally walked in on Roger as he was masturbating and her sex hormones were also running rampant, their parent were away, mother was out shopping and dad was at work, they never had to worry about the help disturbing them. Roger was very much caught off guard, because he and Susan would just come into each other's rooms unannounced most of the time. Susan came over; kissed him and told him not to worry as she gently caressed him as she placed his hand between her legs, they began having one another ever since that day fateful day. It wasn't long after, when they would visit each other bedrooms especially when their parents weren't at home and experiment with one another. They loved each other very much and had expressed to one another often that they wanted to be together forever and once they began having sex their love for one another became so much stronger. Roger didn't like using a rubber but Susan insisted until after they began having oral and anal sex. They became well versed on sex and sexual diseases, knowing more about it than the average adult, or even some doctors. When they were in college, they satisfied one another many times. And they didn't have to contend with other people when the need arose, and spent many nights just sleeping with one another in bed even if they didn't engage in sex. There relationships with others was just a minor disruption in their lives and was more of a show for their parents.

Susan loved her mother very much and they got along very well, as did Roger and his father. When Roger informed Susan of his father's offer of the available apartment next door to the family home, he told her he automatically had a bedroom for her and Susan said she would be happy to be near their parents and have the privacy she needed to be near her brother. Susan had a dark side, if you would call it that, and Roger was the only one who really knew about it and helped her maintain her deepest and darkest secrets, because he truly enjoyed watching his sister, the Mistress Stone perform on her lowly subjects. As a matter of fact Roger had participated with her many times, and at times provided her with some of the most willing and most submissive subjects she practiced her dark art on, and all were women. Susan was a dominatrix and loved subjecting other women to her cruel and dominant side and enjoyed inflicting pain and pleasure at the same time driving her victims crazy. Neither Susan nor Roger could explain when and how they had begun to become involved in B&D and S&M, but it probably began when they started having sex together and Roger spanked her vagina and she had an extreme orgasm, she was surprised and it gradually progressed from there. She liked other women, as long as she could dominate them and soon progressed to a high level of dominance. But she was always loving and somewhat submissive with her brother and would do anything for him, anytime.

Chapter Two

    Roger wasn't any different than his sister Susan, when their mother Ethel Anne asked to speak to him one day and said she didn't want to be to personal or get in his business but decided to asked Roger if he was gay since he hadn't introduced her to any of the possible and very eligible women who he infrequently dated and felt he should or might be considering marrying. Roger laughed and answered, he just hadn't found the right girl yet. But said he was seriously considering marrying Susan, he was in love with her and had been for a very long time. Ethel Anne was taken back and shocked with his answer and commented that really wouldn't be practical. He said they each had different birth parents and it would not be unnatural. Ethel Anne said, but she is your sister. He said yes, but only by marriage. Ethel Anne later had a conversation with Susan. Again this time she asked Susan if she was gay also, and said she had noticed she had a pennant towards females and received almost the same response. Ethel Anne was again shocked when she expressed that Roger would be the perfect man for her, and if she ever married it would be Roger. Their parents were in dismay over the answers both had given when asked and decided to sit down and speak with them both together. They asked them to please reconsider if they were serious about what they had both expressed to them when asked. Their parents said they would someday like to have grandchildren and for them to also consider passing on the family fortune. Roger and Susan said they would reconsider, but also let them both know they were very much in love with one another and had been since they were children. Their parents never brought the subject up again and nothing more was ever said about it. Roger Sr. and Ethel Anne knew they were very close but had never thought about what they had just been confronted with. After the family meeting, Roger and Susan went next door and immediately went and made very sensual and passionate love to one another.

Roger had kept his Sutton Place penthouse since he owned the building they moved from, and decided to use it as a personal play pen for him and Susan. They would stay there often enough but mostly when they had some poor damsel they needed and wanted to practice their perversion on. It has a special large room outfitted for them to practice their perversions in. Roger owned several entire city blocks of buildings in a district that was known for its scandalous and varied underground entertainment venues. Several in different neighborhoods of turn of the century industrial buildings that in most major cities were now becoming gentrified as Roger rehabbed and made them very upscale and was one of the first developers to have done so. Many he rehabbed and turned into luxury condos which helped boost the prices he charged for rents on the ones he retained. He purchased several other similar locations that were scattered in and around the city and continued to duplicate his and Susan's successful restaurant and club ventures. Susan located her first fully exclusive club in one of these multi story well-built buildings with its high ceilings and with its deep turn of the century basement cellar that gave the impression of being in a dungeon because of the large stone work. This one in particular was an exclusive, very private S and M club, called Whips and Chains. Dominant mistresses and masters frequented the club and fully patronized it, and it was a very private members only club with high security and was a highly popular club for the serious practitioners of bondage, discipline, sadism and masochism and operated by invitation only to certain outsiders. The membership was secretive and extremely exclusive and very expensive, $10,000.00 a year for a membership and it included your own private suite and it was available 24/7, and also occupied several adjacent buildings and one directly behind the main building that faced the opposite street and members could come and go unseen and unknown from the public eye at any time. It was the best and most exclusive club for the most serious practitioners, as a cadre of submissive and masochist came or were taken there to please their masters who were club members in its many large public exhibition rooms and private suites. It was one of Susan's dirty little secrets since she owned and operated it exclusively. The other clubs and restaurants on the block, either Susan or Roger owned outright or had an ownership interest in because he owned the properties and they all were very profitable for them both. Susan also opened her first restaurant on the block, Passion Fruit and it had a very upscale clientele, some of who were whips and chains members and would turn out to be the first of many under the same name as it built a reputation of exceptional service.

Susan had several personal maids who she took full sexual advantage of since these women were illegal aliens from Latin American and were totally thankful and under her very dominant control. She also had an Asian girl in her twenties, also illegal and she was also employed as a maid and was subject to Susan's very frequent and sometimes extremely cruel fantasies. They lived on the premises and were well taken care of when they weren't subject to Susan's or Rogers perverse needs. When Susan frequented the club sometimes she would have one or two of her servants with her and sometimes she would put on a show, with the helpless women bound, strapped and tied, whipped and penetrated as she and other masters and mistresses performed for each other in the large open public stage area used for exhibitions and demonstrations in the building cavernous and exclusive basement arena not even open to the public. The private club portions which required the pricy membership were only open to regular club members, and were open well past closing time for the other night clubs. Roger would watch his sister perform her artistic punishments on these helpless women and really saw how much enjoyment it gave her. Roger enjoyed himself also, whipping and inflicting pain on Susan's submissive servants as she watched closely and made suggestions to him.

Then one day Roger met a young woman, very pretty; about five foot nine, and the same age as Roger with a very shapely figure and she had a quiet subdued personality. She was very easy to get along with but had deep emotional problems as a child and that still seemed to affect her some now as an adult. She and her mother were totally dominated by her father even though they were very well to do. She became infatuated and very attracted to Roger, overly so with his strong personality. Susan picked up on her willingness right away and her submissiveness to let Roger control her, even when he made meaningless suggestions. Susan told Roger she would be a good choice for him and possibly produce an heir and satisfy their parents who so much looked forward to being grandparents one day. Her name was Peggy Sue Thomas and her father was a very prominent stock broker. Peggy had met both Roger and Susan at a lavish party given by a competing investment firm and Roger along with his father; mother and Susan were all in attendance at the very opulent and posh affair. Bob and Sarah Thomas and their daughter Peggy Sue all introduced themselves. There was a rather strong an instant attraction Peggy had for Roger as everyone moved about enjoying the festivities, cocktails and food. There was dancing and Roger enjoyed himself and met several attractive and available and also well to do women, some not quite as petty as Peggy, but very wealthy. Roger was taking a break from the festivities and was enjoying the view of the city from the roof top garden as Susan came and stood with him and pointed out Peggy Sue. Susan suggested he should pursue Peggy since she picked up on her very submissive personality and also suggested they both might have some fun with her. Roger knew what his sister meant when she spoke like that. She told him she was really watching him very closely and he should speak to her soon. Roger did as his sister suggested and soon he and Peggy Sue were enjoying themselves and each other very much. Roger talked to Peggy and said she worked in an office as a computer programmer and had a small apartment in one of the high rises nearby close to where Roger had moved from, his former penthouse residence that now was his and Susan's play pen. They exchanged phone numbers toward the end of the night and Roger offered to drop her at home but she declined since she had come with her parents. They said they would call each other as the guest slowly began to depart. Susan and Roger rode home in the family limonene with their parents as they all went home.

It was almost midnight when they both arrived home and Susan and Roger decided it was just too early to call it a night and decided on a visit to Whips and Chains for a night cap. After the chauffeur dropped their parent off at home and they bid them a good night, they were off to enjoy one of the special performances since the famous Master Tong, the world renowned Japanese master of rope bondage was there to demonstrate some Sabari rope techniques. It was a very special show as Roger and Susan very much enjoyed the show as the rope master demonstrated some of his special rope art on three of his submissive slaves, showing how to restrain and restrict movement without cutting off circulation of the limbs and inflicting overwhelming pleasure and pain at the same time. The show was over at three am, and Susan checked with one of her managers before she and Roger returned home. Susan was very excited by the demonstration as conferred with Master Tong and he agreed to come and demonstrate some techniques personally for her the following day at Rogers's old residence where they had set up a well-equipped bondage play room. Susan took the day off and Roger went to work and only stayed half a day since it was a Friday and joined his sister soon after at the penthouse apartment. Susan sent for a car to pick the master up and had brought two of her maids, Maria and Min, and very soon Master Tong had both strung up nude and secured them both as he showed Susan how to suspend them safely without cutting off the circulation to their limbs. Susan was an avid and very adept student and learned very quickly as the Master complemented her on her adept skills and especially on her use of the whip, riding crops and her use of dildos to inflict the maximum amount of pain and pleasure at the same time. When her victims were finally released they were instructed to clean the room thoroughly before leaving. Master Tong would perform again tonight at Whips and Chains and had been provided free of charge with a full service suite for him and his small entourage of three women. He was returning to Japan in the next few days after visiting another major city on the west coast. Roger and Susan after the maids had cleaned everything, returned with them to their family home.

Soon after returning home Min, her Asian maid walked in the room behind Susan and she wasn't immediately aware of her presence and when Susan turned around, she was startled by her presence, and when she saw her flew into an angry rage and was going to punished Min by making her lay prostrate on the floor nude and was about to administer a severe whipping with a leather strap just as Roger came into the room. Roger stopped her as he sensed her anger, and she explained to him what had just happened. Roger suggested to Susan to hang bells on her and then she would hear her coming. Susan told Roger that was an excellent idea and they should pierce her labia and nipples and attach small bells. Susan had Min service Roger instead and then they both had their way with the helpless young woman. Susan lay back on the bed as Min licked Susan and Roger took her from behind vaginally and then anally until they both were very satisfied before whipping the young woman, anyway. When they finished made her crawl to her bathroom and bathe. Roger said he would do the piercings and all they had to do was take her to the play room and strap her in the doctor's chair. They both said they looked forward to doing it and would enjoy her discomfort and decided to do it tomorrow. They had the piercing equipment, needles, rings and bells and would also have their way with her as they punished her even more as they hugged and kissed one another.

It was later that same afternoon when Roger received a phone call from Peggy Sue Thomas. Roger suggested they go to dinner later that evening and she quickly accepted the dinner invitation. Roger informed Susan of his dinner date and she told him that he would have no problems with Peggy, she knew the type and she was really ready to serve him and not to be surprised if she threw herself at him. Susan said she was as ripe as a peach, ready to be eaten, they laughed, and she told him she hoped he had a wonderful evening. Roger said to her they could share her if he decided to marry the poor girl. Susan said that sounded so delicious because she was so very pretty but also very pliable. Roger went and showered, deciding on what to wear, and finally decided to go casual but dressy and wore some jeans and a nice sports jacket, with a pair of loafers. He called Peggy and let her know he was on his way. He had the family chauffeur take him to where Miss Peggy Sue Thomas resided and had him wait as he went inside to her apartment to pick her up. Peggy was so happy to see him as he escorted her to the waiting auto and had the chauffeur drop them off at one of his favorite restaurants, one Susan owned. Peggy was a very beautiful woman with a very nice figure, slim and graceful but under the surface she had a very subservient personality. They talked, she was really talkative now and explained the reason why she wasn't married already, it was because of her very domineering and controlling father who prevented all of her possible suitors from coming close because he said they were paupers and he remained very much in control of her life even now even though she didn't live at home had made her very dependent on him and his wife. One thing for sure Roger wouldn't have that problem and Mr. Thomas would hand Peggy over on a silver platter just to be able to say she was married into the White family.

The dinner with her was very enjoyable and Peggy was infatuated with Roger as he picked up on her neediness and after wards they went for a stroll through the neighborhood and stopped at a popular night club for some drinks and dancing. After a few hours, Roger and

Peggy left the club and he hailed a cab to take her back home. When they arrived he escorted her inside to her door and she asked him in, he declined and told her he had something important to do the following day with Susan and needed to get an early start. Peggy kissed him good night and said she would call him again the next day if he didn't mind. Roger said he would very much look forward to hearing from her again. Roger could tell she was highly excited and wanted him very much but was going to play hard to get since it was the first time taking her out and obvious she wanted a serious and steady relationship. Roger departed as the cab was waiting for him and he soon returned home. He and Susan were planning to deal with Min the next day and Susan was awake as he went upstairs to the patio and had a drink and she soon joined him as they talked before going to bed together.

Chapter Three

The following day Roger and Susan had their breakfast served to them as usual by Maria, one of Susan's maids and one of the three housekeepers as they discussed their planned activity for the day. Susan asked about his date with Peggy Sue Thomas. Roger told her it went well and how right she was about her, but was going to play hard to get since she was infatuated with him. Roger suggested that maybe her and Peggy should engage in some activities together and really see what she was all about. Susan said that was an excellent idea and would really play into their favor especially with her father since he liked to name drop about all the rich and famous people he knew and might probably even help in their future business associations.

Shortly after breakfast they went to their bedrooms and Rose the other housekeeper was making up Susan's bed and cleaning her room and asked Susan if there was anything special she wanted done today. She said no other than her regular duties as Susan prepared to dress in a comfortable but shapely fitting pantsuit. Roger dressed in some jeans and a sports jacket as he met Susan in the hallway and they went to find Min, and soon found her cleaning one of the bathrooms and instructed her when she finished to report to them. Min replied yes mistress, as she departed they went to the living room and had more discussions about Peggy Sue. Susan said she would like to see Roger marry her if she turned out to be what she suspected she was, a submissive that they both could have fun with and could control. Susan suggested Roger be aggressive with her and use some restraints on her before and after he had sex with her several times, and suggested for him to go slow with her and slowly build it up to complete domination . Roger asked Susan if she wanted her based on how she was talking and Susan said if it didn't work out with him she would have no problems making her one of her willing minions. But Susan said she would rather have her serve him at least first instead, but suspected she would be a good submissive and bisexual candidate.

Shortly Min reported to them dressed in her maids outfit as Susan instructed her to go put on a short skirt and blouse with hi heels and no panties. Min left and went to her room as instructed and returned a few minutes later and Roger and Susan then took her downstairs via the service elevator to the second floor and they entered the adjoining parking garage across the bridge between the two building that only residents used and through the secure entrance, exit and quickly walked to where they had several family automobiles parked as they all got in one with Min sitting in the back seat. Roger drove to Sutton Place, the high-rise he owned. They arrived shortly as Roger pulled into the buildings underground garage and parked in one of his designated reserved parking spaces. They all exited as the poor Min had no idea what was in store for her this time as Roger and Susan smiled at one another as they thought about their plans for the helpless but beautiful Min. They walked to the exclusive private elevator for the penthouse only and ascended to the very top floor where Roger still maintained the extra-large duplex penthouse apartment.

They entered the large apartment and went straight to the bar and fixed themselves a drink as they made Min disrobe and stand before them as they discussed what they were going to do to her first. Susan departed to the playroom and returned with a pair of handcuffs, collar and a leash and attached the collar to Mins neck. Susan handcuffed her hands behind her back and returned to the bar to sip on her drink. This was not Mins first time here or her first time being forced to perform for them but what they had in store for her would be a real surprise for her. Susan asked Roger if he was ready and he replied he was as Susan attached the leash to Min and they led her to her to the room where they would pierce her. Roger opened the large tall and wide doors as Susan led Min inside and they entered the very spacious room where there was located a very special chair, one similar to what a gynecologist would have in a medical office. Susan released the hand cuffs and had Min sit in the large chair. This was a very special chair the arm rest and leg rest had straps for securing the feet, knees, wrist, elbows, neck and several for around the waist and chest. Once they had adjusted the chair to fit Min, they made sure she was very well secured. After strapping her securely in they raised it up just by pushing a button like some chairs in beauty salons and doctor's offices and then spread the leg rest to open very wide as the poor Min was now fully exposed and Roger said she needed to be shaved first. Susan asked to do that as she went and prepared a bowl of warm water as Roger first shaved her with and electric razor as Susan soon returned with a large bath towel and a razor and some shave cream. Susan pulled up a stool between the now helpless Min spread legs as she begged Susan not to hurt her. Susan told her to shut the fuck up, and began shaving her with very adept skill, shaving her as Roger sterilized some stainless steel needles and rings and clamps for her labia and nipples and he asked Susan how many rings should the helpless Min have she replied two should be enough for a start now. Roger sterilized the piercing tools and rings and soon was ready to perform his surgical expertise on Min. After Susan had washed and shaved her, she admired her small vaginal lips as Roger rolled over a surgical table with the needed surgical items and took his place on the stool before the wide open Min as Sarah explained to her why after being told repeatedly not to walk up behind her without announcing herself she was going to be pierced and bells hung from her as she began crying and begged her mistress for forgiveness. Susan slapped her hard several times and told her to shut the fuck up you stupid little dumb bitch, as tear rolled down her pretty face. Min knew all too well Susan was very displeased with her to have decided on doing what she was going to have Master Roger do to her, and was totally at her mercy and she dreaded if Susan decided to take her to Whips and Chains again and display and humiliate her again even more. Susan had done that several times before and Min dreaded the experience every time and afterwards was on her best behavior.

Roger put on the surgical gloves and cleaned her thoroughly again with liberal amounts of alcohol before placing the surgical clamps on the small thin vaginal lips of Min. Roger had done this before and Susan enjoyed watching Roger as he cleaned her again with more alcohol and began to perform the piercing like a skilled surgeon. Roger took the special piercing needle and inserted it between the two clamps and made the necessary incision and inserted the needle as he then attached the ring to the needle and pulled it back through as he wiped the blood from around the now whimpering and crying Min. He then prepared to do the other side being certain that they were exactly across from one another in case Susan decided to place a padlock on her vagina. He completed the first task and was shortly done with her vagina as the helpless Min fainted and he cleaned her up with the alcohol again. Susan asked him if they should wake her and he said no, don't bother as he stood and prepared to pierce her nipples, which were very large and long for her small breast size as he decided to use the next size larger needle and rings. He pierced her nipples with no problems and inserted the rings easily in each of them, when he finished Susan placed smelling sauce under her nose bringing Min around. Roger stood back and admired the superb job he had just preformed on the helpless Min taking picture with his cell phone. He went to a nearby cabinet and removed two pairs of small but very loud bells which he then attached one to each ring after dipping them in alcohol. Susan went and removed a dildo from the cabinet and returned with a suction device which she placed on Min very exposed clit causing it to fill the void in a large clear plastic chamber. Susan and Roger went and departed the room as they left the device on Min and fixed themselves drinks toasting there latest accomplishment. They returned and resumed where they had left off as Susan removed the device from her helpless maid and admired the now very swollen and sensitive clit and began playing with it as she applied a large ball shaped vibrator to Mins clitoris bringing her to a huge climax as she held the dildo against her for more than a few minutes until she climaxed and almost fainted again. They released Min from the chair and then placed leather cuffs to her small wrist and then attached her to chains that hung from a bar attached to the ceiling and after attaching cuffs to her ankles spreading her legs apart with a spreader bar and just letting her hang spread eagle before them as they left the room and went and fixed another drink and deciding what to have for lunch. They decided to go to a nearby bistro and have lunch before returning to have some fun with Min, it wasn't Mins first time hanging like this and it had only been a month since she was last in this same room and in a similar situation, only this time she was pierced.

They left the penthouse apartment leaving Min hanging helpless as they headed to the nearby restaurant, they walked since it was only a couple blocks to one of their favorite places to eat and toast their latest endeavor. While they casually walked along looking at the sights and holding hands, Roger received a phone call from Peggy Sue. Said she was lonely and asked where he was, he informed her he and Susan were heading to lunch at a nearby restaurant and told her the location. Peggy lived only about two blocks away and knew the location and asked if she could join the two of them, he said sure, why not and told her they would wait for her outside at one of the side walk cafes and then they would all go to lunch together. Peggy said they would see her very soon and ended the conversation as he and Susan approached one of the many new outdoor street cafés. He hung up and Susan said let me guess, that was Peggy Sue; he said yes it was she. And Susan said her pussy must be burning up and dripping wet with overwhelming amounts of lust. Roger laughed out loud as they took a table outside and he could see up the street about a block as they soon ordered. Susan ordered a latte and he a large plain black coffee. Susan sat and told Roger how much she loved him and said they should marry anyway because he was so perfect for her no matter what their parents thought, he said he felt the same way. Roger could see up the street and less than half an hour later he saw Peggy in the distance. She was wearing a skirt just above the knee and a sleeveless blouse with some hi heels and her hair was loose and flowing down her back. As Peggy neared he paid for their coffees and stood as they then casually walked toward the fast walking and approaching Peggy Sue, and soon greeted her on the street. Peggy was so very happy to be with them, she hugged Roger and then Susan before they crossed the street together to the quiet little bistro that Roger and Susan really they liked because the food was so very good and fresh. They entered and sat at a cozy table and soon had placed their lunch orders. Susan asked Peggy what her likes and dislikes were as far as fashion and engaged her in some small talk as Roger listened intensely to the conversation between the two women. When their food arrived Roger intervened and said time to eat ladies, as the two women slowed their conversation somewhat. Peggy said her father was excited about her seeing Roger and said it was one the first times he had actually told her that someone was a good match for her. Susan smiled at Roger and he knew what it meant since they were so very close in more ways than one. They ate slowly and when Roger finished before Susan and Peggy he pulled out his phone and brought up the camera app for the penthouse. He saw the helpless Min as she began urinating on the tile floor and thought she would have to lick it up and passed the phone to Susan, she looked and said no she didn't and said to Roger she going to have to lick it up as they both laughed. Peggy looked at them and wondered what they were looking at and asked what was going on. Roger said they had to discipline one of their maids because she had disobeyed Susan and this wasn't the first time since she had been warned, and the punishment she was suffering, had been long overdue, and now she was just hanging around, as he and Susan began laughing at his snide remark. This kind of remark really excited Peggy and she asked if she could see, and Susan nodded for Roger to show her. He handed her the phone and she gasp, but looked at it a very long time and was enthralled with what she saw. Then out of nowhere she said that she had always been severely disciplined at home by her father many times. She went on to say he disciplined her mother also, and from an early age she taught to obey her father without question. He would whip her mother when she wouldn't listen or talked back to him or didn't do as she was told, he would use a belt on her then take and have sex with her, having his way with her and tried to hide what he did to her. Said one time when she disobeyed her father and he was really very upset with her, he tied her to her bed face down naked with her legs and arms spread eagle and whipped her and afterwards she couldn't sit for down without pain for several days. But after that she was so turned on afterwards she climaxed when she masturbated thinking about it. She caught herself after what she had just said and apologized saying she didn't mean to let that out and felt embarrassed by her comment. Roger said it was quite all right, and then said you understand what happens to insolent servants and that is what he and Susan had to take care of so it wouldn't happen again. Peggy had the look of real understanding on her pretty face and said she fully understood. She asked Roger if she did something he was displeased with would he punish her. Roger stated if they were married he wouldn't hesitate to punish her and the same applied if they were going together to make her into a very obedient wife and would give her both pain and pleasure at the same time. Peggy blushed at the thought of what Roger had just said to her as Susan sat back and thought how Roger had now just let the cat out the bag but then again maybe it's what she secretly wanted as Susan observed Peggy pressing her knees tightly together as a sign of being very highly aroused and excited.

They had finished eating and Roger asked Peggy if she wanted them to walk her back home. Said she would rather spend the day with them if they didn't mind. Roger said they were going back to the apartment where the maid she observed was hanging. Peggy seemed a little hesitant at first but then she wanted Roger very much and would do anything he wanted if he asked her. Their invitation excited her and Susan could tell she was ripe for exploitation and started getting ideas about what to do with Peggy since she was so infatuated with her brother. Peggy expressed a willing desire to go with them since she didn't have anything else to do. On the way back Susan's phone rang and it was a call from their mother asking if she had plans for the evening because her and their father were going to dinner and wondered if they wanted to accompany them. Susan declined and said Roger was with her and they had other plans and the conversation ended. Susan explained what the phone call was all about. Roger said well they could go anytime and what they had to do was more important anyway.

They walked back to the apartment and entered the building and rode up to the penthouse on the private elevator. Peggy was in complete awe when she entered the beautiful and very spacious modern lobby of one of the most exciting new apartment buildings in town and even more so as they entered the private elevator to the spacious top floor unit. When they arrived Roger offered her a drink as she marveled at the view from the balcony sixty-five stories up with a fantastic view of the park and city scape. They fixed drinks and Susan asked her after she finished her drink a short time later if she was ready to watch her punish her unruly slave. Peggy said yes and became highly excited as Susan and Roger led her to their special play room, in a section of the spacious apartment where their play room was located and where they had left the helpless Min hanging. When they entered Min was again struck with fear and urinated again as they entered, Roger and Susan laughed. Susan walked over and said you know bitch, you will have to lick all that up as she slapped her face, but not until I whip you for doing it. Min began to cry because she knew Susan could be extremely cruel at times and was a real talented master with the whip. Susan walked and opened a cabinet that was filled with various styles and types of whips and chose one that would be very painful but would leave few lasting marks. Peggy was starting to get highly excited and scared at the same time as Roger went and retrieved a pair of hand cuffs from a drawer and returned to where Peggy was standing watching Susan and without her being aware of him being behind her took her by surprise and cuffed her arms behind her. Roger whispered in her ear not to say anything but just watch, she began to get even more excited now as Susan pulled back and whipped the helpless maid and shortly changed whips and whipped her as the newly installed bells rung. Susan whipped her between her legs until she had another massive climax and then walked over to Min and asked her what do you say slave, and she replied in a weak halting voice thank you mistress Susan as tears ran down her face. Susan unhooked her ankles and then her wrists as Min collapsed on the floor in her own urine before making her kneel and start licking it up off the floor. Peggy was so excited now that she asked Roger to please touch her private parts, and when he placed his hand between her legs, her panties were soaking wet as he played with her and she soon climaxed. Her hands were still cuffed behind her when Susan walked in front of her and said to her you want to please my brother, she said yes please, and Roger undid the handcuffs and Susan told her to undress which she didn't hesitate in doing.

Susan told Min to lick her shoes you little piece of shit as Roger threw a rag down for her to mop up the remaining urine with and when she finished made her kneel and observe what was about to happen to the now highly excited Peggy Sue. Susan placed the cuffs on Peggy and suspended her from the same bar where Min had been hanging, and then placed the cuffs on her ankle as well and then the spreader bar. Soon Peggy was panting with excitement as Susan stood in front of her and licked her face and told her to kiss her back which she did without hesitation or resistance. Susan reached down and felt Peggy's moist vagina and knelt down to take a closer look and saw she was soaking wet and her vagina was small and tight but she had a gap between her legs then stood and walked behind her and spread her ass cheeks. Susan walked back in front of Peggy and asked her if she was ready to serve, and she said yes, Susan said what bitch, as she lightly slapped her face and Peggy said yes mistress. Susan said that's better bitch. Susan asked her if she was ready to serve both Roger and her and she said, yes mistress. Susan said very good and asked her if she wanted to be punished, she replied yes mistress again.

Roger sat back and prepared to let Susan work her magic on this willing submissive and maybe his possible future wife. Susan blindfolded Peggy as the anticipation in her really built up and went a found a whip that would really bring excitement to her quivering body. She whipped her all over as she circled her before taking a wide strap and whipping her between her legs from in front and then from behind as Peggy erupted in a huge long lasting climax before just hanging almost limp as Susan removed the blindfold and looked into her beautiful eyes kissing her. Roger came forward and felt her and she quickly came again as he whispered what he was going to do to her. It was his turn as he went and brought back a couple dildos and some lubricant as he released her legs and smacked her ass hard several times and told her to stand up you dirty slut, he liberally applied some of the lubricant to her anus as he wore a surgical glove and ran his finger deep inside of her virgin anus as she now moaned with pleasure as he worked it around inside of her until he had two fingers inside of her tight anus as he kissed her and she kissed him back, then he slowly inserted an worked the large dildo into her anus and worked it back and forth as he continued to kiss her, after it was inserted several inches up inside of her he took an even larger and longer one and inserted it into her now sloppy wet vagina. Peggy's frown soon turned into a startled look as she had another massive climax unlike anything she had ever experienced before in life as Roger kissed her and she kissed him back. He went to a cabinet and returned with some large clothes pins and placed them on her now swollen an aroused nipples as she moaned and massage her vagina and clitoris with his hand as she now shook uncontrollably as her body was racked with multiple organisms before he slowly worked the dildo in an out before removing it from her anus and twisting and pulling the large pins on her nipples as he slowly removed them, then he released the cuffs from her arms as he held her now overcome with sexual pleasure limp body in his arms and Susan helped him take her to the bedroom where they laid her in bed as Roger and Susan undressed and then rubbed on Peggy's now limp and exhausted body. Then Roger and Susan made love to each other as Peggy watched laying weak and helpless next to them before they took Peggy, as Susan sat on Peggy's face and rubbed her vagina roughly against her face until Peggy responded and when Susan climaxed in her face Roger took his turn as he filled her vagina with his large penis and poor Peggy climaxed again. When they finished they took Peggy to the walk-in shower and they both urinated on her as they made her kneel and keep her mouth open before making her lick both there asses. They stood her up and turned the water on and bathed her like you would a child. After they finished, they took Peggy back to the large bedroom and rubbed her down with massage oils. Peggy was totally weak and exhausted from being used. Roger went to check on Min and she was where they had left her and Roger brought her to the shower and made her bathe before he placed her in bed with Peggy and ordered her to oil herself and Peggy.

Roger and Susan then ordered some food to be delivered for all of them and would decide on what to do next with Min and especially Peggy. Susan said she didn't know Peggy was such a willing slut and thought they should have her and Min put on a show for them, Roger said that sounded really great. An hour and a half passed before the food arrived and when they went and checked on Peggy and Min found them both sleeping together. Susan woke them up, and made them come eat but first handed them both robes as Roger and Susan fixed there plates. Roger asked Peggy before she was allowed to sit down who she belonged to, she said she belonged to him and his sister and would be very good. Susan smiled when she heard Peggy's answer to Rogers's question. They all sat and ate and when they finished had Min clean up. Min had been here before and knew where and what to do. Roger told Min to report to him after she finished cleaning up. Roger, Susan and Peggy had drinks that Roger prepared as they sat on the couch with Peggy in between them. They both kissed on Peggy and they told her she belonged to them now, she was their slut as they felt on her, getting her very aroused again as Roger told her to get down on her knees which she did without hesitation and told her to suck him off, and after she had accomplished that told her to eat Susan's vagina which she soon did without hesitation, when Susan climaxed she raised her ass up and told her to lick it, Peggy complied and did as she was told again without any hesitation what so ever. When she finished and Min returned they had Peggy between them and made Min lick Peggy's vagina and anus as they both hugged her and when Peggy climaxed they had Min lay on the floor and Peggy eat the prostrated Min and told her to do whatever she wanted to Min. Peggy had Min on her hands and knees as she spanked her and fingered her pussy making her climax as Susan and Roger watched her and said let's make this a little more interesting as Roger went and returned with a couple dildos and a whip and gave them to Peggy and told her to use them on Min.

It was a wonderful sight as Peggy inserted the dildo into Min tight little anus and another in her vagina as she made her crawl around as the tiny bells rang out and she whipped Min as she crawled around. Roger went and fixed him and Susan another drink and returned to the couch as they hugged and kissed and watched as Peggy whipped Min. Roger stopped Peggy as Min lay crying and he pulled her by her hair and made Min suck him off and then lick his ass as she thanked her master for the privilege. He ordered Peggy to bend over the end of the couch as he began whipping her and asked her who he was and with tears in her eyes said he was her master. He and Susan took Peggy and Min back to the showers and made them bath each other as they watched. When they finished escorted Min and Peggy to a bedroom and made them oil one another again. Roger and Susan showered together and then oiled one another. They made Min and Peggy sleep in the same bed with them as he and Susan called it a day, since they now were all fully exhausted.

Chapter Four

When Roger woke it was early Sunday morning, he looked over at Peggy who was lying between him and Susan, with Min next to her. He went to the bathroom, returned and woke Min up. He instructed her to clean herself first and then begin fixing breakfast. She got up and promptly followed Roger instructions as he also told her to get one of the maid's uniforms and put one on. Min departed to do as she was instructed as Roger returned to bed and woke Susan. She rose and immediately went to the bathroom before returning as they stood looking down at Peggy lying asleep in the large bed. They hugged and kissed one another and put on their robes and left the room. Min had fixed the coffee as they sat and had a cup before she started fixing breakfast for all of them. Susan said she really enjoyed what they had done yesterday and said now that Peggy seemed to be theirs; they would see when she woke where her mind was really at. Roger said she just gave in to their wills so easily, and said to Susan you said she was ripe, and said she was over ripe by his standards and offered little to no resistance. He suggested they wake her as they headed to the bedroom and she was still sound asleep when they woke her up. Peggy rose and the surroundings were unfamiliar to her until she saw Roger and Susan standing over her and then remembered yesterday and where she was. She rose and hugged Roger, then Susan as they handed her a robe as she went to freshen herself, before they said it was time for breakfast. When they entered the kitchen Min was just finishing up and fixed their plates as they all sat down to eat and told Min to eat with them as Peggy entered and sat down. When they finished eating Min cleaned up and Roger told her to finish by cleaning the apartment but to first change the sheets on the bed first before cleaning elsewhere.

Peggy stood and hugged Roger and said she loved him and asked if he would be her lover as he reached under her robe and held her tight and said as long as she was obedient and did as she was told. Said she would be and only wanted him to love her. Roger told her she would have to love and obey Susan also if she wanted him. Then he asked her if she loved Susan, to which she replied she loved her also. Susan stepped over as Peggy turned and hugged and kissed her. Roger asked Peggy what he and Susan should do with her today and she replied whatever they wanted she would do as long as Roger was with her. Roger suggested to Susan if she would demonstrate some of her Sabari techniques on Peggy since she was so willing. Susan said how very delightful and thoughtful as they led Peggy again to the playroom where Susan began removing the soft ropes from a cabinet and when Peggy removed her robe Susan began tying her expertly with the ropes. After half an hour Peggy was securely hanging from the bar above with both arms above her head and the rope laced around her body as her breast were made to bulge out and with one leg suspended behind her. Roger took several pictures of her as she hung suspended and Susan marveled at her handy work. Soon Susan placed her in another position and Peggy was enjoying being the object of their attention. They spent half a day tying and retying

Peggy and Roger must have taken a thousand digital photographs as Susan performed her rope magic on her. When Susan finally released her she flew into Rogers arms and asked him to take her because she was so excited from the rope bondage.

Roger led her to the bed room where she asked him to spank her as she had her arms around his neck. He kissed her as she pleaded and said please master, to make love to her after he spanked her, he had her kneel in the bed with her ass up and head down, arms stretched out in front of her just as Susan entered the room and handed him a short wide heavy leather strap, Roger smacked her buttocks lightly several times after rubbing the strap all over her beautiful body before striking her lightly, then harder until her ass cheeks started turning red. When he stopped he rubbed them and pulled her up by her hair to face him as he looked in her now tear filled eyes, slapped her before he kissed her and she kissed him back passionately as he moved his hand between her thighs and she quickly climaxed as soon as he touched her and wrapped her arms tightly around him. He laid her on her back and climbed on top of her and entered her beckoning vagina as she moaned and said she loved him and climaxed again. Roger pulled out and bent her legs back holding her ankles, and entered her anus as she cried as he slid into the tight orifice until he climaxed inside of her filling her with his hot sperm causing her to climax again. Susan then climbed in bed and sat on Peggy's face as she now licked Susan with passion until she climaxed in her face. Peggy was satisfied now as Susan climbed off of her bending over and kissing her.

They then took Peggy to the shower and lathered her up as Roger had his way with her again, fingering her anus until he had three, then four fingers inside of her and Susan fingered her vagina and soon Peggy erupted with a massive climax as Roger then entered her anus with his penis again as Susan played with her as they held her, after she climax they bathed her and themselves and then dried her off and led the weak and helpless, but very willing Peggy back to the bedroom where they continued to molest her body this time using massage oils. Susan went and returned with a harness, collar and leash that they easily attached to Peggy. It had a large but soft butt plug and a short latex penis and it fit between her legs easily and also around her waist. Susan placed a collar she brought around her neck and a pair of leather cuffs that attached to the sides of the harness. Susan attached a leash and they stood the helpless but very willing Peggy up and led her around the large apartment and led her outside onto the expansive outdoor terrace and made her stand in the sun exposed to the world as they fixed themselves drinks and returned to gaze at her as Roger took more photos.

Peggy was completely physically helpless as they sat and gazed at her, speaking epithets and insulted her as she soon began crying. They became cruel in their treatment and after a half hour later they led her inside as Roger took even more pictures of her as they continued their verbal degradation. They continued walking her around as she became more and more aroused again but could do nothing to relieve herself of the pleasure or discomfort she was now feeling. Roger approached her and asked her if there was anything she wanted. In a halting voice she said please could he feel her she wanted to come. Roger said you have to ask in the proper way bitch, she said please master will you feel me please, Roger looked into her pretty but pleading face as he smacked her on her ass several times as she jerked and began climaxing violently. Roger had to hold her up as she was rocked with multiple climaxes. As they subsided he made her sit in a chair as she almost passed out. Susan was laughing and said she is truly a real slut and wondered if her mother was the same way, and then blurted out, like mother, like daughter. They allowed Peggy to get some self-control before Roger made her stand then kneel in front of him as he sat and asked the exhausted and sexually overcome Peggy if she was now his bitch. She said yes sir master as he pinched her nipples and she moaned and jerked, as they soon heard Min cleaning and her bells ringing. Roger made her stand as he released her arms then removed the harness handed it to her as he instructed her to lick it clean which she did without any hesitation. Susan went and brought back a robe for her and wrapped Peggy in it and led her to the couch where she held her and wiped her face with a damp wash cloth, Peggy now was like a baby in Susan's arms. Roger sat next to her and they pampered and petted her, and told her they loved her and that what they had done to her was to see if she was worthy to be a part of their special family. Peggy asked if she was and Susan kissed her and said she was now, and then Roger kissed and held her.

After almost an hour they said it was time to go out
and eat, and Roger suggested they dress and walk to a
nearby restaurant. Susan and Roger had clothes here as
Susan took Peggy to her bedroom and asked her if she
wanted to wear something different. Peggy was ecstatic
that they accepted her as Susan said that she couldn't
wear any panties or a bra, but had to wear her hi heels
and to be careful what she chose because Roger would be
upset if you were exposed when you sat down. Peggy
chose a skirt that fell below the knee and Susan said
excellent choice. Soon they were ready and Peggy had
combed her hair and placed it in a bun, and had applied
some makeup, not much and some lipstick. Roger was
dressed casual as he escorted the two beautiful women to
the private elevator for the ride downstairs.

They entered the lobby and walked to a nearby
restaurant as Roger walked between the two sexy women
and about a block away they entered the Town and
Country restaurant, one of Susan's own restaurants. They
were immediately seated at the reserved booth as the
waiter presented them with the menus and Roger ordered
a bottle of red wine, as they studied the menus. By the
time the waiter returned and poured the wine they were
ready to order. They placed there orders and the waiter
departed. Peggy was sitting facing Susan, as she sat in
the corner and Roger was next to her by the isle. Roger
placed his hand on Peggy's thigh and felt between her
legs as he licked her ear and told her she belonged to him
now as she turned and said to him yes sir master. Said
she wanted to be with him all the time no matter how he
treated her. Susan knew what Roger was doing and told

him to stop, which he did as he looked at her and said ok sis. Susan said she's yours and you will have plenty of time to play with her. Soon there food arrived and it looked and tasted very well as they all ate and enjoyed the sumptuous meal. They ordered desert afterwards and when they finished Roger paid for the meal and they departed and walked to the park, it wasn't far as they went for a short walk and Roger took some more photos of Peggy and Susan before they all returned to the penthouse.

They had Peggy gather her clothes from yesterday and said they would walk her home. Peggy said she didn't really want to go home, but Roger insisted since tomorrow was Monday and he had to go to work and Susan also. They reassured Peggy she was now part of their special family, even though Roger hadn't asked her anything yet, like being married. Peggy reluctantly said ok, and after placing her clothes in a small bag they departed again as they both walked with Peggy the four blocks to her residence in a fairly modern building as they went upstairs with her to her small apartment. It was a studio apartment, small, but very clean with plenty of sun light in the day time. Roger and Susan kissed her and told her they would keep in touch with her. Roger and Susan departed and walked back and talked about their busy and erotic weekend with Peggy. Susan told Roger he should marry her one day soon because she was someone they both could have fun and sex with and she was such a willing submissive. Roger said yes, I think you might be right. They went back upstairs and entering the penthouse could hear the bells on Min as she

continued cleaning. They ordered her to the play room
and into the chair as Roger checked on her piercings and
cleaned and rotated them and he instructed her to clean
the area around them twice a day and also again after she
bathed. They told her to get dressed as they were
returning home and checked that she had cleaned as she
was instructed and was very satisfied with her work.
They departed and headed downstairs to the garage as
Min rode in back as usual as they returned to their
primary residence.

Roger parked in there designated parking space and
then they walked back across the upper bridge and
entered the mezzanine and went upstairs after entering
their private elevator. When they arrived at their
apartment Susan said she had a wonderful weekend and
reminded Roger that Peggy doesn't know that we don't
live at Sutton Place, the name of his building where he
had moved from but still had some clothes there just as
she did. He said I know. Susan said I hope she doesn't
just try to just drop by if she gets lonely or feels the need
for our presence and that he should inform her not to go
there. Roger said when he called her later this evening he
would let her know. Roger soon called Peggy and told
her that was where he used to live and not to just pop up
because he and Susan stayed elsewhere and that she
should call if she felt the need to see them. Peggy said
she would always have a need to be with them and loved
them both but she understood. Roger said he loved her
and bid her a good night and said he would try calling
tomorrow if he wasn't too busy, and hung up.

Susan told Min to come to her room and instructed her not to wear any undergarments or panties so she could hear the bells and as a matter of fact to wear just an apron when she did her house work, she said yes mistress as Susan dismissed her. Susan called Maria and Rose and said that if they disobeyed they would suffer the same fate as Min and asked them if they understood. They both responded yes mistress, as she then dismissed them. Roger went up to the upper level and fixed himself a drink after taking a nice long warm shower and sat and enjoyed the outside air as Susan soon joined him and sat on the wide chase lounge with him as they talked as he felt on her and told her how much he loved her. Susan said she was glad Peggy was the way she was because she was prepared to be with them and was glad they could share her. After a couple drinks they went inside and went to bed together for a much needed rest.

Chapter Five

The following several months seemed to pass quickly after him and Susan had Peggy that fateful first weekend, the beginning of many more to come as things started turning out extremely well for them both and became especially beneficial for Roger as he acquired and closed on several large buildings. He was now slowly and methodically expanding his now growing personal real estate empire which now consisted of ten large properties, with some being very prominent, six of them were office building and the remainder were residential and was in the process of consolidating his real estate operations from being run as separate entities into one corporation and allowing him to have even more of a financial leverage with the banks. Out of the ten, four were some of the most modern in the city and they were all forty stories or more with Sutton Place being his tallest. He decided his new company would be named ROWE. Which were his initials and would give him the ability to raise even more capital based on his combined holdings along with Susan's now ever expanding restaurant business. His last purchase was a very large old warehouse and manufacturing site in a neighborhood that was being redeveloped now into an upscale residential area from an industrial one of a by gone era as technology was changing the face of manufacturing and the architectural landscape in many older and large cities around the world, as heavy and light industries moved further out from the city centers into large or medium sized suburban industrial parks with better transportation access. The older and very well constructed buildings of yester year presented many new opportunities because of the more durable materials that were used in there sturdy construction and created several special opportunities as they were repurposed and rehabbed with modern technology and amenities. Many were built to support the extremely heavy machinery of the past before the age of plastics, composites and other new light weight materials. Roger purchased mostly all of his many properties outright, and very much preferred buying them that way so he would have total control, and converted them into the best use and had been very successful profit wise turning several into large loft style condo apartments and would and could make up to ten times the original purchase price on many occasions once all the rehab work was completed depending on the varied sites and locations, and having completion in a reasonable time frame of little more than a year or so. He also had purchased a large thirty eight acre factory site and the large dilapidated warehouse across the street that sat on another twelve acres. They both were in such a poor condition it wouldn't have been practical to rehab either one and decided to just demolish both and use the thirty eight acres it was on to build a completely new development from the ground up as he put several bids out to several architects to come up with ideas consistent with best usage and what he envisioned for the location and space. The site across the street would be developed along with the larger one. Soon he had varied concepts presented to him that consisted of several low and hi rise apartment and condo buildings complete with ample parking and plenty of retail space. This project would take about three to four years from start to finish or maybe even longer before completion since it was in a prime redevelopment corridor. Roger would take his time developing the property and would add it to his new company's now rapidly growing and much diversified real estate portfolio.

His father admired him very much but hadn't really been obvious with his admiration and asked him one day what he was doing since he seemed to be very preoccupied as they sat down and talked. He asked Roger what he planned to do when he inherited the reigns of the White company one day. He said he didn't know since he was now more involved in his own small business enterprises and they would remain separate and would decide what direction he should take them in at a later date. His father stated he would like to see him merge some of his assets into the White Company but only knew about a couple of properties and wasn't aware of Rogers's recent and extensive holdings, and stated they could still remain separate. Roger said he would rather keep what he had separated until all his new ongoing projects were completed. His father then asked him if he had found a woman yet that he might consider marrying. Roger said he had but hadn't asked her yet. His dad smiled at him and said he was going to promote him to the upcoming vacant third vice president position and asked Roger if he would accept the position when the current third vice president retired. Roger asked to give him some time to think about it because he had a lot of projects he was working on right now. His dad said that was fine with him as they shook hands and he asked

when he would he get a chance to meet the lucky girl.
Roger said maybe very soon, as they ended their meeting
but not before Roger asked him what part would Susan
play in the company. His dad said she would become
head of departments because she had her law degree and
one in finance and she could be his number two when
and if he took over the vice president position.

Roger said he had the upmost confidence in Susan
and her abilities and that she had some very profitable
business ventures of her own. His dad frowned and said
yes I know. Roger asked him just what he knew about
her business ventures. His dad said he knew about her
ownership in the Whips and Chains club, and knew it
wasn't you average social club. Roger said so you know
then and he said yes. Roger said he owned the building,
and his dad said yes he knew about that also and some of
their other combined business affairs. Roger told his dad
he loved Susan very much and was very happy having
her as a sister and would marry her if he really wanted,
but knew him and mother frowned on the idea and that
was the only reason he hadn't done so already. His dad
hugged him and said yes son I have known for quite a
while but he said he wasn't trying to run his life, but said
you need to produce some heirs because he and his step
mother were looking forward to one day of having
grandchildren running around and he was the one they
felt most likely to succeed in that area. Roger thanked his
dad and departed his office as they went their separate
ways and soon returned to his own.

Roger texted Susan and asked her to meet him for
lunch. She texted him back as they set a time and place.

It was near the end of the week and Roger had spoken to Peggy several times and said he would maybe see her again this weekend, and she had spent several weekends together with him and Susan over the past several months. Roger and Susan met for lunch and headed to an exclusive restaurant not far from work. Susan looked superb in her blue pinstriped business suit with her short skirt with stockings and hi heels and Roger in his dark blue pin stripe suit as they entered the restaurant and were shown to their reserved table right away. It was when Roger told her about his conversation with Roger Sr. And what he said he knew about their love for one another, and what he had told his father about how much he loved her and how he would like to marry her. Also about how he knew about her involvement in the S&M club, and that he owned the building and several others on that block. Susan said she wasn't surprised and he would never tell mother on them, or maybe she knew also. Susan said it didn't matter anyway and maybe it was better they did know and said they want grandchildren more than being concerned with their love for one another or their expanding business operations. They ordered their food and Susan asked when was he going to introduce Peggy to mom and dad. He asked her if this weekend might be too soon. Susan said no it wouldn't because Peggy was more than ready to do anything he or she wanted, and besides she came from a respectable family and nothing would change that. When the waiter brought their food they started eating. Susan said if Peggy was acceptable to mom and dad then we should bring her into the company. Roger said he would offer her a job at ROWE since he was still looking to expand his now very small staff, since he only had three people so far and would soon need an experienced programmer and a much larger office. Susan said that would be a smart move brother, because as a family member she would have a vested interest in the success of the operation, if she is qualified. Susan asked him where his corporate office would be located, he said he hadn't decided yet and would check with dad about some office space in our building, and if it wasn't available he had a plan in the works now and was just waiting on an answer. He pulled out his phone and texted his dad and said he needed to meet with him again. Dad texted him back and said sure around three this evening would be fine.

They finished lunch and Roger said he would wait and see if Peggy was accepted by mom and dad before he made the next move. Susan said that's a smart move and would be the best way to approach the situation as she paid and they walked back to there offices. Roger asked her to attend the meeting with their dad since he was going to make her CFO of their new company ROWE, she looked at him and laughed and held his hand and said she loved him as they kissed and hugged before walking back to work. They went to their offices and it was soon three o'clock as Roger went to get Susan and then together they went to their father's office. His secretary had them wait as he was finishing up a meeting that was running a little late. When he had concluded his business conference, Roger and Susan were led into the office by his secretary and said he was sorry the meeting was running late as they both took a seat. Roger said he had thought about their earlier discussion and he was here to ask him some specific questions. The first one was, if there was any available office space in the building he was willing to rent or let them occupy. Roger said he was considering whether he should let his newly reorganized company to possibly become a subsidiary of the White company. Roger said the assets would have to remain separate for the present time. This presented his dad with a problem because he wouldn't be able to leverage the assets of the new company the way he wanted. Roger Sr. asked what part Susan played in the company. Roger said she was CFO and he was CEO. The new company had very solid assets; they weren't fluid and would soon rival the White company, only they were hard assets. Roger Sr. said that wouldn't work for him and he would have to think about it for a few more days and would give them and answer soon. The office space wasn't available because it had been rented already. Roger and Susan stood and he said it was just an idea, thanked him for his time and they departed.

As they departed Roger told Susan he had an office building he was hoping to purchase and had placed a bid on it a three weeks earlier and told her it was the one right across the street. It was so much newer and Roger said he would place large letters in front on the large plaza and rename it the ROWE building. Susan laughed as they walked away. He said dad had only the time it took for the seller to accept his latest offer.

The next day, that Friday evening Roger received a call from the seller's agents for the building across the street. His latest offer had been accepted, Roger was truly overjoyed and phoned Susan right away and told her, and she said good work brother. He immediately phoned his dad and informed him the offer from yesterday was off the table, and thanked him for his consideration. ROWE would be a privately held and wholly owned company and would be owned by him and his sister, and now would have offices across the street in a modern ten year old glass and steel; sixty nine stories, building that had suffered from low occupancy rates because of, bad management, high rents and very poor maintenance. Roger made a low bid for the building but it was a cash offer and Roger was ready to close within two weeks and put his legal team on the job. His legal team was him and a couple of legal aids that he now had working for him and of course Susan. They had done this together before and would be ready to close in two weeks. He called his dad again and said, maybe this weekend they would get to meet the new woman in his life and would let him know but he had to go because he was very busy and hung up.

Roger called Peggy and asked what days this weekend she would be free, and she said whenever he wanted her she would be where ever he wanted her to be, before he asked her about her job. She had on a couple occasions when they were out talked about her job but that was very seldom, since he and Susan weren't interested and didn't pay much attention, since they were into taking full advantage of her submissive sexual ways. But now Roger was getting ready to pull off his greatest business feat yet and needed very experienced and loyal people around him and besides he was going to show her off to his parents for their stamp of approval. Peggy explained that she was a computer programmer and would organize files and operating systems and had a degree in the field and in a couple of others. Roger asked her how much she made, she said almost fifty thousand a year but it was actually much less and her dad supported her some financially. He told her to fax her resume to him today and he would call her later tonight and hung up soon after giving her the fax number. Susan came into his office and said she was going to move her club and restaurant operating offices also after they acquired the new office building. Roger said good and you can then pick the space you want and told her he wanted to be located on the lower floors. She said good move because you could easily leave if there were any mechanical problems. She asked about the purchase price and what the financial terms was this time, and asked Roger how he was going to pull this particular real estate deal off. He said he valued the building at over two hundred million, but only offered sixty million cash and would refinance the existing outstanding debt of another sixty million. She said that doesn't leave you stretched out does it. He said no way, only for a month or two he would only have about fifty million cash and that was a combination of operating funds and reserves, but the condo conversion would soon be wrapping up in a week or two and sales had already started and was well on its way of being sold out in a couple more weeks. And the demolition had been completed of the building across the street from it and would soon be breaking ground for the new complex down the street from it in the next few months, and all of his apartment and office buildings have now have exceeded a ninety five percent occupancy rate. And beside I have you to back me up in a real pinch. Susan said her management company had just posted there quarterly profits and she was now making slightly under two million a month in profits. She told Roger she was getting ready to open her sixteenth restaurant and the newly instituted card program was now a month old and working really well and was beginning to take off and was racking up more profits and they were bound to increase. She told Roger the four night clubs were cash cows and was going to soon rename and consolidate her management operation and rename it, it would soon be known as Suzanne Enterprises. Roger started to speak again as his fax machine started printing Peggy's resume. He told Susan that he was thinking of hiring her and placing her in charge of organizing the different departments. He removed the fax and read the four printed sheets and then handed them to Susan after he finished reading them. He said look at that, she has a bachelors in business, computers and finance and is a CPA, and is only making fifty grand and has seven years of business experience. Susan said give her an interview right away so we can really talk to her. Roger called Peggy thirty minutes before she was due to leave work and to set up and interview for her for Monday morning at ten, but then told her to call once she was home. Peggy said she would as Roger said he had to go.

Roger and Susan prepared to leave, but first walked across the street and crossed the expansive plaza to their future home offices and entered the large expansive lobby. It was very spacious and well lite with sun light and looked at the buildings directory and decided to go up to the second floor and found it completely empty, the space had been stripped of all office equipment, even the carpeted areas were bare concrete now and was wide open, they went to the next floor up and found the very same thing. The next floors were occupied before they decided to go to the very top floor and found only half the space occupied. They rode down and wondered again as Roger looked at the directory. The building was less than half occupied and Roger stopped a few workers as they stepped off the elevator and asked them if they had a minute or two to answer some questions. He asked if they liked working here, and mostly all said yes, but said management was slow to make and respond to their maintenance request or complaints, and when he stopped one man who turned out to be the head of his company he told them the rents were to excessive for the poor service and lack of competent maintenance, and he was going to move his operations very soon if things didn't change soon since he had heard the building was being sold. Roger asked him for his business card and told him he would soon be talking to him again. Roger shook his hand and introduced him and Susan. As he left Roger turned to Susan and said this is going to be the place to be in six months just wait and see. It had a prestigious address and was in an exceptionally good location, and besides it was across the street from the White Company.

Chapter Six

That afternoon after Roger and Susan arrived home and started to unwind and relax; he showered and soon fixed a drink. Peggy called, and soon Roger asked her to come have dinner with him and Susan and he would send a car for her. Roger called the family chauffer and asked him to pick up Ms. Thomas and gave him the address. Roger asked Susan where they should go to dinner and she suggested the Silver Club, it was one of Susan's establishments and she kept a reserve table at each one of her restaurants. He said good choice and he really liked the food. An little more than an hour later there was a knock at the front door and Rose answered the door, it was Peggy as Rose showed her into the living room and said Mr. White would be right in and asked her to have a seat as she went to inform Roger that his guest had arrived. Roger soon entered the living room as the awe struck Peggy stood and hugged him. Peggy said she missed him and Susan so much. Peggy was dressed in a comfortable summer dress with open toe sandals and her long hair was braided in back. She wore no bra and told Roger she loved him and then asked him why he wanted her resume. He asked her to sit down as he sat next to her and started to explain why, just as Susan walked in looking stunning in a black evening dress with hi heels and no stockings and came over and kissed Peggy. Peggy told her she looked stunning and was very beautiful and said she wished she was as pretty like her. Susan said to her she was pretty also, she just needed a little work.

Susan asked if they were ready and Roger said yes, as they left the apartment and entered the hallway just as

Mrs. Ethel White stepped off the private elevator and Roger introduced Peggy to his mother. His mother said such a pretty girl Roger; I hope you treat her nice and said how lovely it was to meet her as they entered the elevator. They had the chauffer take them to the Silver Club; they soon arrived and were shown to Susan's reserved booth. A waiter promptly appeared and took their orders as Roger began to explain to Peggy the position he wanted to offer her and said since he looked at her resume she was more than qualified for the job he was offering her and the pay would be two hundred thousand a year. Peggy was stunned and sat speechless as Roger began explaining to her what she would be required to do and then asked her if she would accept the position. Peggy's mouth was open but no words came out right away, and when she finally did, she said yes. Susan explained that she would be required to oversee her restaurant operation also as part of being employed by them and for another two hundred thousand dollars and asked her if she could handle both positions. Peggy had finally realized what was now happening and said yes to both offers. Roger said he would give her two weeks before she would have to officially fill the position but should be available as soon as possible since he and Susan had a bit of work to take care of before everything would really start falling into place. Explained that the office space was vacant and would need to be furnished first and it would take some time but needed her to review the present operational setup and then get everything organized or reorganized the way he and Susan had envisioned it to be and she could confer with them on any needed changes to the operation to make it as efficient as possible with the least amount of expenses and employees.

Peggy's business-like manner began to appeared as she said that after Monday she would be available and would want to get started as soon as possible and would like to see how he and Susan were operating now and then she would be better able to present a plan and give it to them within the coming week. Susan said that sounded very good and said there's was a multimillion dollar operation and couldn't afford any mistakes and were depending on her abilities to follow through on their expansion plans and it would be very beneficial to her also. She thanked them for the job offer and finely said she accepted. Their food arrived and they ate and talked more as they could see her mind hard at work and said they loved her and it was one of the reasons why they had chosen her and besides she was more than qualified.

They began eating and Peggy didn't talk much, and Susan asked her what she was thinking about, and she said all they had just said to her and how she was going to accomplish it. Peggy said it was such a total surprise and it would take her a little while to digest it all, as Roger smiled and said it will get easier. Told her he and Susan wanted her to spend the weekend with them and go to dinner either Saturday or Sunday with them and their parents. Roger asked her if that was acceptable to her, she said yes it was and Susan said they would go shopping tomorrow for some new clothes and she could keep them at their apartment and she would have her own bedroom also. Peggy smiled and asked when Roger was going to ask her to marry him. Rogers jaw dropped, and Susan laughed and said she isn't stupid brother. Roger just looked at her surprised, and said soon my love. Peggy then said she would accept his proposal whenever he decided to ask.

They finished eating and Susan handed the waiter her new club card and he returned with her card and a receipt. They decided to go to one of Susan's clubs as she explained to Peggy she owned the restaurant and Roger the building they just ate at and now were going to the 500 Club and the same thing applied there also. She owned the club and Roger the building and had just started issuing membership cards to qualified persons who applied using the same criteria as a credit card company and it would be billed to them directly or to a bank account or a credit card and covered all charges including a built in tip. And that she would automatically receive one and it would be billed as a business expense. Peggy said she understood as they hailed a cab and went to her club. The 500 Club was an exclusive club and you could tell by the people and how they were dressed as they entered and Susan and Roger were greeted by the doorman as they went to another reserved booth and watched the people enjoying themselves as a waitress appeared and took their drink order. They only stayed a short while and they soon returned home and went to their apartment and showed Peggy her new bedroom before Roger took Peggy next door to their parent's apartment as Susan stayed behind. They were let in by the maid and went to the living room and soon both Mr. and Mrs. White came in and Roger introduced them to

Ms. Peggy Thomas. Roger Sr. said he knew her dad and complimented her on how beautiful she was and Mrs. White told her to call her Ethel or Anne which ever she preferred as they all sat and talked a short while. Rogers's parents liked her as she was intelligent and had poise and was very graceful. Roger and Peggy spent almost an hour before they returned next door.

Roger and Peggy then went and sat on the expansive terrace and talked as Roger told her he wanted to get his operation up and running before he would formally ask her for her hand in marriage and asked her if she understood. Said that she did and understood. Roger said she shouldn't say anything to anyone about their marriage yet, not even to her parents. He told her he wanted her to move in with him and Susan but only if it was what she really wanted to do and would give her time to think about it. If she did decide to move in he would have it done before the coming week was up as he looked her in the eyes. They held each other as he felt between her legs and her panties were soaking wet and told her to take them off, which she did without hesitation. Roger felt her and asked her who she belonged to, and she said you master as she climaxed and he held her tight. Then he led her to his bedroom and he undressed her and told her to kneel in the chair as he spanked her ass before he plunged his penis deep inside of her from behind as she soon climaxed again then he stuck it in her ass and he climaxed shortly after. He led her to his bathroom and they showered together as he asked her about birth control and she said she didn't take any. He said after they were married he would come inside of her so if she became pregnant they could have some children. She told him she didn't want to become pregnant quite so soon and he would just have to continue climaxing in her mouth or ass. He said he understood and was glad she didn't take the pill because all he had read about them they were harmful. She told him that's why she didn't use them and beside he was the first man she had sex with in more than seven years and was very happy it was him. They finished bathing and went and oiled one another and put on some robes and went upstairs and had some drinks.

Peggy said she had three months left on her apartment lease and then she would move in with him but needed time to think about all that had just happened between them the past few months and especially today. Said she loved him but didn't want to feel like she was rushing into a relationship so quickly and the job offer was also going to be a challenge all by its self and hoped he understood. Roger said he did and that she was doing the right thing because he wanted her to be sure about everything and said it was a lot to swallow at one time. But he said at the restaurant you said if I asked you would. She said yes, she had, but would still want to take her time and said she loved him and wanted him to really and truly love her and fully understood his deep love for Susan and she loved her as well and wouldn't stand between them ever, and truly understood how much they loved one another and was willing to be her lover also as long as he was with her and in her life. They finished their drinks and went downstairs to his bedroom climbing into bed and hugging and kissing until they fell asleep together.

Susan had left out again to make the rounds at all of her night clubs and restaurants checking on the various operations and making observations and making her presence known and being visible to her employees. She did this at least once a week now and at various times and on random days. She called them popups and made sure things were going her way. She had been to the 500 Club and Silver Club with Roger and Peggy so no need to go back as she hit the Rock House, Executive Club, Town and Country, Uptown, Passion Fruit, No.10, Paton Place with her last stop being, Whips and Chains. She was accompanied by her body guard and was driven by her personal chauffeur. Both were on her payroll and were on duty from 6pm until. She only spent a few minutes at her last stop before going home and releasing her two employees for the night. She went to her room, showered, fixed a drink and then went to bed. Tomorrow was Saturday and planned on taking Peggy shopping something she really liked to do, and would dress the girl up and make Roger drool and then plan an evening out with the family.

Chapter Seven

That morning when Roger and Peggy woke, they hugged and kissed one another before going to the bathroom together to freshen up, and soon returned to bed. He pushed her down in the bed on her back and asked her who she belonged to, she replied to you master, as Roger spread her thighs open and entered her as she kissed him madly and soon climaxed, before he turned her over and holding her arms behind her back entering her vagina again. She quickly climaxed again before he pulled out and assaulted her anus and climaxing himself. They lay together holding one another for several long minutes as Peggy said she would serve him and Susan faithfully. They went back to the bathroom to shower and Roger bathed her and felt her again causing her to climax several more times as they made love again. They dried off and then applied lotion and oils to one another before dressing. Roger then led her to the dining room where breakfast was just beginning to be served by Maria and Rose, just as Susan joined them. Susan kissed them both before sitting down as they began eating. Peggy said she really enjoyed being waited on since cooking wasn't one of her most favorite task. Susan said she had the day all planned, she and Peggy would go to her apartment so she could change and pick up some clean clothes she could keep here and asked her if that would be ok and work for her. Peggy said yes, it would. Susan said after they finished eating they would get started but she had to dress first since she was just wearing a robe. Susan asked Roger what he was going to do and he said look over some of the plans and paper work for the new office building and start working on their reorganization, then maybe later go for a walk. Susan told him she would need him to be available this evening because she had planned a dinner with their parents. He said he understood and wouldn't get too lost.

Susan excused herself and said she would be back as Peggy asked if Roger had an extra toothbrush, they went to his bathroom and he handed her a new one from his bathroom cabinet. She unwrapped it and brushed her teeth and then he brushed his and afterwards and they kissed. Before Peggy left Roger took her in his arms hugged and kissed her and told her she was his and loved her, she kissed him back as she became excited again and said yes master as she almost climaxed in his strong arms. He released her and Peggy went into the hallway as Susan appeared and they both kissed Roger and left for the day. Roger went to the study to revue his operations and made extensive notes and looked at his financials and figured out his strategy for operating the new office building and which of his leasing agents he would place in charge. He also started looking at possible future tenants he could make offers to with discounts on some office space. Or on long term leases for short periods and decided if an advertising strategy would be beneficial and spent several hours working until he called Rose. He informed her of what he wanted for lunch as he continued working and Rose soon brought him his lunch. He finished his sandwich and went and washed his hands as Rose returned for the empty dish and thanked her before returning to continue with his work a little longer before he was finished. Then went and fixed a drink and then lay down and took a short nap.

About three hours later Roger woke and it was close to three when he changed clothes and checked his phone and there were no calls from anyone important and cleared the memory and unplugged it from the charger. He decided to go to the park and take a walk after taking a quick shower and then maybe Susan would have returned with Peggy and thought now about how much he missed them both. He dressed and went downstairs and crossed the street and had walked several blocks and before he knew it he was looking at one of his buildings, and when he looked down the street he could see another one of his properties. Just as he decided to head back home, his phone rang. He looked and it was Susan as he answered. She asked him where he was, and told her that he had decided to go for a walk in the park. Susan said they were home now and that he should return. He told her he was heading back and hung up. Roger headed back but not before he stopped at a book and magazine store where he picked up a couple copies of the local business news magazines before he continued walking back toward home.

He rode up on the elevator to his apartment and entered and dropped his magazines off in his study where he had been working earlier before looking for Susan and Peggy. He found the door to Peggy's new bedroom closed but could hear voices and laughter, he knocked and the door opened and Susan said about time. He entered gazing upon who he thought was another woman as she turned around and faced him, but it was Peggy.

She was dressed in black stocking, black open toe hi heels, with a black sleeveless evening dress trimmed in gold around the hem, arms and neck with a single wide shoulder strap, her hair had been done in and upswept style that became her beautiful face, she wore some makeup and lipstick and her nails and toes were done. A gold chain with matching earrings complimented her pretty face. She poised for Roger, she didn't look at all like the same girl that had departed earlier that day, but was the most beautiful woman Roger had ever seen besides Susan. Susan had turned her into the most stunning picture of beauty ever. Roger looked at her and just stared at her transformation. Susan told Roger they were going to dinner with mom and dad and to go put on something presentable. Roger was so awe struck he said you are so beautiful and left the room to go put on a suit. Roger returned with a nice suit with a knit shirt and continued looking at Peggy. Susan said I bet he will ask you now. Peggy said he has, but said they were not ready to make any announcement yet and to keep it a secret. Susan said ok she would.

About half an hour later after they were all finished dressing and ready, there was a knock at the front door and it was Mr. and Mrs. White as they entered the apartment and went directly to the living room and then Susan and Roger along with Peggy in tow entered and said good evening and that they were ready. Mrs. White was in awe at the sight of Peggy now and reached for her hand and kissed her as Susan said lets go as they all soon departed. Roger and his dad followed the women out of the apartment to the elevator. Susan had planned the evening with a semi private room at one of her best restaurants, the Silver Club and had the wait staff on standby. They exited the building to the family limousine that was waiting to take them on the short ride to the restaurant. Susan led the way followed by Mr. and Mrs. White, then Peggy and Roger. People's heads turned as the group entered and several people took pictures of them, one in particular was a columnist and restaurant critic for one of the large local newspapers who recognized Mr. White and Mrs. White due to their philanthropic causes and were well-known being important and wealthy semipublic figures.

Susan's staff knew this would mean a lot to them and provided the group with the royal treatment. Mr. White didn't know Susan owned the restaurant and Roger the thirty story and extremely well maintained building the restaurant was located in. When Roger Sr. had dropped on him that he knew about Susan's night club ownership she had only the one club and one restaurant when he did his last investigation of their business operations. That let Roger know it had been several months since he had looked at their overall holdings, but then again the way they were organized now was kind of hap hazard and was what he and Susan were working on now and would soon change in a few weeks. Roger had held each property separate until his recent formation of ROWE a couple weeks earlier and they still weren't really visible to just the cursive investigations Mr. White might perform and didn't really know how extensive the empire was the two of them had built and controlled since and were continuing to build and would be in for a real shock when

Roger acquired the office building across the street from The White Company very shortly.

The wait staff was really extra attentive to the White party and Mr. White complimented them but had no idea that the reason why was because he was sitting with the owner and CEO. Their orders were taken but everyone was in awe of Peggy's transformation as Mrs. White had Peggy's ear the entire time. Roger was so proud of what Susan had done and told her so. Susan reminded him that Peggy had to look the part for her new job as the executive director of ROWE. Roger said you are so right sister and he told her he had spent most of the day working out how they would proceed and had several outlines and would go over them with her tomorrow. Mr. White looked at them and asked what are you to cooking up now and they said oh nothing much. Their food arrived and they were served by three waiters. They began eating and the food was superbly well prepared and very tasty. Susan took out a small tablet from her purse and wrote on it and then signaled a waiter who was nearby and handed him the note, it was for the manager and it read, well done with her initials on it. It would mean a nice bonus for the entire wait staff, and that was how Susan had been able to retain the best people to work in her establishments and all were known for their very courteous and superb service. As they finished eating the table was cleared and the desert menu passed around. Roger and Susan and Mr. White ordered desert but Mrs. White and Peggy abstained. Coffee was served to all as Mr. White said he had never experienced such excellent service before in a restaurant and would be sure to bring his business associates here for lunch. Roger just looked at Susan and smiled.

They prepared to leave and Susan handed the waiter her Club card and they returned with the card and a receipt as they prepared to depart and Susan paged the limousine driver, and he was waiting at the curb when they exited the restaurant. Susan had planned the entire evening and they were taken now to the Uptown Club for cocktails and dancing, it was a club for the well to do older and mature set. It was a very well appointed and had a lavish decor and was very laid back but had a dance floor and a three to seven piece orchestra every evening after seven pm and sometimes a vocalist would accompany the band and they would sing some of the classics. It was a favorite of many wealthy older couples and most of the patrons were well over thirty. It was an exceptionally nice club and Mr. and Mrs. White even got up to dance as did Roger with Peggy and then Susan as he complimented her on planning such a beautiful evening for them all. She said just for you brother and our family, and said dad has no idea he ate at our restaurant and is dancing in one of our night clubs. Susan said I am glad he knows about Whips and Chains because he doesn't have a clue or know too much about our business, and when we open across the street he will be in for a real surprise if not a complete shock. Roger said yes he will and said he had offered him the position of third vice president, when the position becomes available. Susan laughed and said oh how wonderful, then said we will make White and company a subsidiary of ROWE instead of the other way round. They both busted out laughing as they returned to their table. Everyone was having a great time and it was near midnight when Susan paged their driver again. Susan used her club card again and was again handed the customary receipt before they departed.

Everyone had a marvelous time and thanked Susan for planning such a lovely evening. Arriving back home Mr. and Mrs. White hugged and kissed them all as they headed to their respective apartments. Roger, Susan and Peggy spent no time undressing and putting on some casual clothes to lounge in as they headed upstairs to have a drink and then sit on the large terrace together. Roger and Susan hugged and kissed one another as they laughed and then hugged and kissed Peggy as they sat and relaxed and told her what was so funny to them earlier. When Susan finished informing Peggy about the complete operation and their dad comments, Peggy laughed and said what a shock it will be when he finds out. She also explained about the card she used and it was the one she had mentioned to her before. Roger told Peggy, he wanted her to resign her job Monday and decided that Tuesday they would start and he had made some changes. He decided he would make Peggy executive director of ROWE and explained to her what it stood for, Roger Oliver White Enterprises, but would always be referred to as ROWE and company, and her salary would start at five hundred thousand and he was going to advance her half Tuesday on her first day and tomorrow they would start going over some of the most important details. And said I know everyone has seen how you appeared in the past, but Monday I want you when you resign to dress like you did tonight and I will be with you when you do. Peggy kissed him and yes, yes, yes and said thank you so much. He said they haven't paid you well and haven't given you any respect and I can't have that for my future wife to be. He went on to tell her during this period he and Susan would be assisting and guiding her and all she had to do was ask as she planned out the new operation and that Suzanne Enterprises would also come under her direction, but Susan would always be directly involved and he would also. They needed her to oversee the staff and organize the office, and said tomorrow they would work out more of the final details as he proposed a toast to the new ROWE Company. They had a couple more drinks and then they all went to Rogers's bedroom and after some hot sex and a quick shower and some sensuous rubdowns climbed into bed together with Roger in the middle and went to sleep.

Sunday morning when they awoke Roger kissed and touched them both before going to the bathroom only to return and found them hugging one another as they both went to the bathroom together as he dressed for breakfast. When they came out they hugged and kissed him and he said after breakfast they were going to get started and it was going to be a very busy day. They dressed in some comfortable clothes as Rose and Min served them their breakfast. When they finished and had spent some time freshening up, they headed to the study where Roger outlined the plans they would follow the next several weeks and described what he had planned in mind. He said that after they took Peggy to her soon to be former job, they would take her around to the various buildings and introduce her to all the building managers and staff and let her observe the way things were operating now so she could better organize their new consolidated real estate operation and would also show her where Susan's small staff that handled the restaurant operations were located and how her operation was running. Then show Peggy the proposed new office space for all their current operations. It was soon time for lunch and they took a break and returned again after lunch and resumed as Peggy took notes and looked at Rogers outlines and said after tomorrow she would have a plan to follow and then begin putting it in place. They worked until pretty late in the evening until Rose came an announced dinner was ready and they decided to call it a day. They ate, and then relaxed again on the terrace and looked at the city from their strategic vantage point over the park and enjoyed each other's company. Later that evening Peggy said she wanted to see the new office space tomorrow or as soon as it was possible since they had told her they hadn't closed and didn't have possession yet. Roger said it shouldn't be a problem. They had some drinks and decided to go to bed so they could get an early start knowing it would be a long and very exciting day.

Susan said she wanted some sex before they turned in. She and Roger engaged in some steamy sex along with Peggy now as part of their exclusive group. They all showered together before going to bed and sleeping together.

Chapter Eight

That Monday morning was the beginning, the very first official day in the creation of the newly formed ROWE Company. After waking up and preparing for the day ahead and after having a wonderful breakfast together, Peggy asked if she could type her resignation on Rogers's computer and then print it out. Roger said for sure, as he and Peggy went into the study where she quickly typed it out, then placed her resignation in an envelope Roger handed her, and made two copies and signed the one she would present to her soon to be former boss, at her very soon to be former job. When she finished, she stood and turned to Roger, kissed him and said she loved him very much and wouldn't disappoint him or Susan in their new endeavor. She said thank you and asked him to please give her a moment as she returned to her bedroom to dress and make some last minute fixes to her overall appearance. She returned with Susan following closely behind. Susan said she would also spend the day with them, since this was the first day in the creation of their new company, and soon to be an even more lucrative enterprise. Peggy said she welcomed the escort and would enjoy the shock and awe she expected it would produce on her old job. Roger called for their car and they soon entered the elevator for the trip downstairs and out through the main lobby to their waiting limousine.

About forty minutes later they pulled up in front of Peggy's very soon to become former job, entering to the gaze of mostly everyone around them as they entered the second rate office building. Roger was wearing his power suit, a black pinstripe, with a solid grey shirt with a gold striped tie, and black wingtip shoes, and an expensive watch and Susan was looking exceptionally beautiful with the full allure of wealth and power and had on a matching blue pinstriped business suit with a light blue blouse and matching short skirt with dark blue stockings and blue hi heels, with a matching blue purse, gold necklace and earrings, as the short skirt accented her very shapely and sexy legs. And Peggy was now the epitome of beauty as all that was hidden before was now visible as she wore the black dress with the single wide shoulder strap, belt with a large gold buckle, with a matching necklace and earrings set, sheer black stocking and open toe high heels also with a matching purse, her long hair was in an up sweep style and rolled in back, and her makeup was flawless. They rode the elevator up to the seventeenth floor and went down a well-lit fairly short hallway to the Harbor and Associates offices and entered. Peggy was then greeted by the awe struck receptionist who didn't recognize her at first as she said good morning mam. Peggy said good morning Jan and continued walking with poise and determination as she headed to her department as Roger and Susan followed closely behind her and directly to her soon to be former boss's office. She knocked on his office door before she entered. She said good morning Mr. Wine as he looked up at her in great surprise and didn't recognize her right away because of her now striking appearance, but soon recovered and said you're late in a derogatory voice, and told her it better not happen again. Peggy said yes sir, it wouldn't as she then introduced him to Mr. Roger White and Ms. Susan Stone and handed him her resignation letter and said it had been a pleasure working here but had been offered a much better position with so, so much more money. He was now showing the signs of getting highly upset with her, as he suddenly stood up, and said you can't quit now, you are in the middle of one of our most important audits and I need you, he said I will pay you more money. Peggy said how much more, he said five hundred dollars more, she laughed and said it couldn't compare to what she had been offered and said thankyou it's been a pleasure and goodbye, Mr. Wine.

Peggy casually strolled to her old desk and acknowledged her coworkers before she reached and removed her lucky rabbit from her now old desk and a pair of her prescription reading glasses from a drawer and a small black note book and placed all inside her large purse. She gracefully turned to Roger and Susan who had followed her and said she was now ready to leave. She said good bye to mostly all of her close coworkers as she waved to several across the large work area and departed and told a few she would be in touch. Her former boss being surprised and now highly upset followed them the entire time and out to the reception area as he begged her to stay, he said please don't leave you are the best person I have and I very much depend on you. Roger turned to him and said, yes she was your best and now she will be my best and will be compensated for her very high caliber skills and much, much more. Her now former boss was now so very, very upset and really pissed off just by Roger and Susan's presence and was really beginning to lose it when he suddenly said to Roger, just who in the fucking hell are you anyway. Roger calmly turned around and faced him and said to him that Ms. Thomas was going to be managing director of the new ROWE Company and he was the CEO and this is Ms. Stone and she is, CFO and if you aren't prepared to pay Ms. Thomas five hundred thousand dollars a year then I suggest you just turn around sir, and go back to the scrubby little hole you just crawled out of that you call an office, thank you. Roger turned back around and said ladies, as he held the door open for them and they departed, as Peggy's former boss was now in shock and very, very pissed off and sick at the same time as he turned, red in the face and just stood and watched them walk down the short hall, and just watched them until they entered the elevator before he returned to his office. He had never been spoken to in such a demeaning manner before, but he brought it on himself. Peggy's former office was now all a buzz after she had left with Roger and Susan and then when lunch came around and the receptionist told some of the staff what had happened. Some of the staff being curious had also entered the hallway well out of sight and had seen and heard the entire encounter and told what had happen in detail also and what had been said in the reception area as it spread through the office like wild fire, they were all truly amazed, and did you see how Peggy was dressed, she was the talk of the office for the rest of the week.

Roger and Susan took Peggy around and toured all of his buildings rental offices before lunch; there was only the ten of them so far and it didn't take very long since several were in close proximity of one another. Susan suggested they go to lunch and took them to the 500 Club for a really fantastic meal. After lunch they went to the small basement office operation that Susan used as her headquarters in a brownstone close to Whips and Chains. It was modern and well-furnished and had the latest computers. After five minutes there Peggy asked to see the new office space. Very soon they were at the building as the limousine pulled into the buildings spacious circular driveway. They exited the vehicle; as they looked out upon the large and spacious plaza that lay before them. They walked around some as Peggy looked up at the modern building before entering the soon to be new headquarters of the ROWE Company. After entering the spacious three story tall lobby and looking around they went up to the second floor. As they stepped off the elevator, Peggy said this is more like it as she walked around the large open sun filled space before they went up to the third floor and she walked around it also. Peggy said that she needed to sit down and talk to them about what office configurations they wanted. Roger turned to Susan and said maybe we should go home since all of his notes and documents were there in the home office.

Susan and Peggy now were in total agreement with his suggestion. Peggy asked if they would stop at her apartment and said she wanted to pack another bag before they returned and they said sure that was no problem. Soon after leaving their future headquarters their limousine pulled up in front of Peggy's building as Roger and Susan again accompanied her to her small apartment and she began packing a large suit case she had with mostly all of her cloths. Roger looked around and Susan said you might as well bring it all because there wasn't very much left. Peggy looked around and decided on taking all of her remaining clothes as she emptied all her drawers and Roger told her they would come back for the rest of her other belongings very soon when she was ready. Peggy said the other day I said not so soon, but I see things are happening very rapidly now, but things do change. They went downstairs and the driver placed Peggy's bags in the limousines trunk, as they now headed home. Peggy told them on the way home they need to plan a layout for the now open unobstructed space, and that they each would need an office, and there should be a space for record storage and asked were they going to have one floor or two or more. She stated the Suzanne operation would need a much larger space now since Susan had instituted the card program, there was going to be a need for and accounts department and the whole operation could just move and be in a more conducive work space and it would make the employees more productive. She also suggested a central warehouse for all the restaurant supplies and operations and they needed to find a suitable location or build one from scratch to suit the operation in order to cut cost and have timely delivery and would need to see all the restaurant locations and talk to the managers. The real estate operation was fairly simple compared to the club and restaurant operations and just needed a space for the records, freeing up much needed space inside the rental offices and having the rental applications checked and processed from one central office location. And the leasing office for this office building itself would become the central rental office for all the locations. The existing offices would act as satellites offices and accept the applications for their location and function the same way they do now since they actually came in contact with the tenants and act to a certain degree in the screening process of applicants.

Peggy said that she would give them a rough drawing of the work space layout and a blueprint and also a guideline for the operations and which ones to put in place first but said one floor would be more than sufficient for the entire operation for right now. But recommended keeping the other floor available should additional space be needed or they decided on more separation after they settled in and smoothed out the kinks in the current operation. They soon arrived at home and the driver unloaded the bags from the trunk of the auto, and Roger extended the handle of the largest bag and Peggy the smaller of the two as they entered and went upstairs. When they entered the apartment Susan called Min and told her to take Mistress Peggy's bags to her bedroom and unpack her clothes and put them away. She also told her to call her mistress from now on, yes mistress, Min responded as she departed to fulfill her assigned duties. Susan then called Maria and Rose and informed them on how to address Peggy also from now on; they said yes mistress and returned to their duties. Susan and Peggy went to their respective bedrooms to put on some more comfortable clothes as Maria came and asked when Susan wanted dinner served and she said at six. Peggy was changing her clothes and freshening up as Min placed her clothes in the closets and drawers and

Peggy asked her to hang up her dresses up and Min said yes mistress, which surprised her and asked Min why she had called her that and Min went on to say mistress Susan said she was to address her as such, Peggy said ok then. Roger couldn't wait to change and was the first one to enter the study and sat down and began sketching out a rough floor plan and would soon contact and consult an office supply company to set up the new office under Peggy's very able direction.

He was soon joined by Peggy and Susan. Peggy began the planning session by suggesting what would be needed first in an office, and for each of them. She suggested that a receptionist, secretary would also be a much needed plus. Said with Susan's operation and the four people she had now was a good start, but may soon need to expand after moving and that would be determined by her new card program. In a short time she would be able to determine if a staff increase would be necessary. Roger said they were already incorporated under the new name now and had been for the past two weeks so the technical and legal portion had been completed and basically moving in and setting up the actual physical space was what was important now and would be needed very soon. Both Peggy and Susan agreed with him and stated they wanted a waiting area and both agreed on having a receptionist. Peggy said she had a few close associates at Harbor that would be more than happy to leave for the right amount of pay if they needed any more really and truly experienced and very reliable employees. Roger said great but we should wait until we get the physical space set up first and everything up and running the way we want first. Peggy said she agreed with him. Roger reminded them they were actually the board of directors as they discussed setting everything up and should also remember that.

Maria came in, and it was six and said dinner was ready to be served. They all went and washed up and prepared to eat and decided to call it a day. They spoke more about the new operation over dinner and tomorrow would deposit into Peggy's account her first half years salary. But he and Susan told her they had to go back to work tomorrow at the White Company because they didn't want their father to find out what they were really planning and had been up to these last past several months. After dinner Roger went and brought with him to the terrace the two magazines he had purchased that past Saturday and started reading them and soon ran across an article in the local real estate market section of the changes taking place locally and who the major players were. There was a mention of a new company that had just been formed, the ROWE Company. The article went on to say there wasn't much known at this time about who was involved or behind the new company or who held the assets or even what they were or even where there offices were located, but promised they would have more about it in the future. He finished the article as Susan and Peggy joined him and he handed the article to Susan and said let Peggy read it also as he opened another magazine and this one had a special article about the local restaurant and club scene. This one was more interesting as it mentioned the 500 Club, and the Executive Club restaurants and said they were some of the best if not the best for outstanding service and the food was excellent and recommended them as a must go to as far as restaurants and club goers were concerned. It went on to say they were part of the newly formed Suzanne enterprises chain and they had just introduced a new diner's club card that could be used at any of their restaurants and clubs and said they were beginning to almost become too numerous to mention here. It said it was proving to very popular with regular dinners because it included a built in tip. There was no mention of ownership which turned out to be very good because they knew his dad read both magazines. He passed the article to Susan to read as she smiled and said she knew the card would pay off big time.

After Peggy finished reading the first article she read the entire magazine and passed it back to Roger and said you might want to read this. The article was about two companies that wanted to move into downtown from their suburban locations to be closer to their client base and were looking for some premium office space. Peggy suggested sending out some feelers and to pull them in quickly since he would have the prestigious address in a few days. Then Susan passed her the article on the restaurants and she read the entire magazine, Peggy was a speed reader and handed it back to Susan and had found a restaurant for sale that wasn't far from one she already owned and the building it was in was for sale also. She said they should at least look at it, as Roger read the small add. Susan said Peggy was a great addition to their operation and Roger agreed with her. It had gotten late and Peggy said she was going to check out her new bedroom and get acquainted with her bathroom and would go to bed after taking a shower. Roger and Susan told her good night as she came and kissed them both and said thank you and that she loved them before leaving and said see you in the morning. Roger and Susan agreed that she was very sharp and would do well running things for them and might just help expand the company they had slowly and meticulously built. Roger said he was turning in as he and Susan went to their respective bedrooms as they kissed and he said he was very tired after such a long day. Susan retired for the night also to begin again tomorrow. Little did they know one devious person was just beginning to have sleepless nights, the first of many more to come?

Chapter Nine

The next several weeks that passed was most uneventful for Roger and Susan as they worked at the White Company and took care of their own business as in the past except when they returned home. But for Peggy, she turned the library, study into the new corporate headquarters and the base of operations for the new ROWE Company. She didn't own a car and had never had the need for one until now, she had her driver's license but since Roger had three and Susan had two, and Susan had her driver, slash, body guard available for her during the day since Peggy was setting up the new centrally located warehouse for all of the restaurant operations in a fairly new building that was designed to operate as a warehouse and transit terminal, Roger leased the building on terms that he would purchase it within a year. Peggy spent her time going through the records of each property and found several discrepancies and made notes and brought them to Rogers's attention every night when he came home, and made her recommendations, which he followed to the letter. Peggy had all the rental information streamlined and in a more precise and orderly manner. Once she had that organized and under control she spent every day for a couple weeks at the Suzanne offices and soon had all the records there streamlined and reorganized. Susan had informed the staff that Peggy was the executive director of operations as Peggy prepared them for the move to their new headquarters. One evening Susan took Peggy with her on one of her spot checking ventures and told her she had tried to do this at least once a week and had tried to pick random days for her surprised checks, Peggy was surprised, but began getting a better feel of the organization and told Susan it helped a lot and would like to go with her more often.

By the second week after Peggy had virtually moved in completely with them both, they had closed and had taken possession of their new headquarters and the very next day Peggy and Susan met with the office supply, equipment and internet computer people as Peggy showed them what she wanted and where and the following day the space was being cleaned and painted. Building maintenance was shaken up as Roger found out from the building maintenance staff that the previous owners didn't want to spend the needed money on repairs and that changed right away, and within a month all the building backlog of complaints had been cleared up as Peggy now ran the building, she interviewed prospective tenants and made arrangements for their move ins. Peggy sent feelers to all the new prospective tenants and former tenants and after three weeks when the new offices opened they were busy signing up even more new tenants. Suzanne had moved into the new space and the employees from Suzanne were very happy with the location and had more room, with all the main offices on the second floor and Peggy kept the third floor empty for future expansion but sealed off the area. Peggy instituted a new diner's card accounts department with two additional people as she pulled several of her former highly qualified coworkers from Harbor and Associates and they helped set the new department up, it was a very efficient operation. There was a receptionist who directed visitors and informed the proper people of their arrival and business. A month after opening the new office the thirty foot tall letters ROWE were installed in the plaza and the building soon gained the reputation of being one of the most prominent locations to have as your downtown office located. Roger was elated as the accounting slippages were now nonexistent with Peggy's diligence, determination and expertise. Even Suzanne enterprises accounting was so much better organized and the staff was happy and paid more and on time, than they had been in the past, and the restaurant suppliers were happier as payments and deliveries went more smoothly. All the different and varied restaurant locations around town now received more timely deliveries with the central warehouse in operation and a new small fleet of dedicated delivery trucks. Profits were now up and three months after closing the occupancy levels had risen past seventy five percent as some companies with just half a floor space were consolidated and compensated for moving and changing floors as Peggy brought in clients who occupied more than one floor and had their central and even international headquarters located here. The building's lobby was redecorated and now was always busy with people entering and leaving as the new owners turned the entire place into a beehive of activity.

It was seven months, almost eight after closing on the building when Roger sat down in his new office and Susan entered and said to him its Peggy's birthday next week and asked him what was he was going to do about it. Peggy had several months earlier moved her remaining few possessions from her apartment and informed the building management she was not going to renew her lease. Roger said he didn't know it was her birthday and had forgotten with all the action and excitement going on around him and Susan and asked him if he needed any help. Susan reminded him she had saved them two million dollars just by reorganizing the real estate operations and also her restaurant operation by stopping the slow drainage and leaking of funds. She told him she also deserved a pay raise and she would take him shopping to help him find a gift for her if he needed some help. Susan said she was going to increase her portion of her salary by a quarter million and suggested he do the same, he agreed with her and also said that last restaurant location she picked out was a real boon for our business and the building was a hidden gem also and was a real steal. Susan also said its time you marry her or she might try and get away from you and then she would have to claim her.

He asked Susan to take him shopping for her birthday gift, she said sure thing, anything for you brother. Peggy had been so involved that the only time they had sex with her the past few months was maybe on the weekend and then she was so tired they just slept with her. He and Susan slipped from their offices at the White Company and headed out and Susan took him to a very prestigious jewelry store and informed him he couldn't go wrong by buying her some nice jewelry. Roger selected and Susan agreed as he chose a diamond necklace, earrings with a bracelet set that cost him two hundred thousand dollars, and Susan said she only deserves the best. Peggy had drastically changed the way she dressed from when she had worked at Harbor and Associates from the average looking frumpy young girl next door, to one of sophistication and wealth and now dressed like a very professional business woman and Susan made it a point to take her shopping at least once a week and together they formed a very strong personal relationship and became the best of friends and lovers. Several days before Peggy's birthday, Roger with Susan present got down on his knee and formally asked Peggy for her hand in marriage. Peggy began crying and hugged him as she accepted his proposal as he presented her with a beautiful diamond engagement ring. They soon went next door together and he informed his parents, they were very elated, and congratulated the couple. Susan immediately began planning a combination engagement, birthday party for her at the now very famous and now prominent 500 club. The big day was going to be a Saturday and all of Peggy's friends, family and associates were invited along with Rogers and Susan's closest friends and family.

It was a gala affair and was semi private with about a half of the restaurant being set aside for the affair and was held in the early evening hours. It was her birthday and when Roger presented his soon to be wife with her birthday gift Peggy couldn't stop crying and wouldn't let go of Roger. Susan had to console her as Peggy said she never thought she would be so happy and lucky and asked Susan to please stay with her as they hugged. Later that evening when it was all over and they went home, Peggy wouldn't let Roger leave her side and followed him all evening and night and said she had always loved him as he just held her until she fell asleep in his arms.

The following day was a Sunday and they went for a walk in the park and when they returned home Susan had the new monthly issues of the local real estate market and restaurant magazines and began reading the reviews and as she finished handed them to Roger. Susan said you should read these, and then told them the cats out of the bag now. She told him to read the local street beat article on page twenty-one. Roger turned to the article and it was an in-depth full page story about the new ROWE Company and there extensive real estate holdings and was a closely held and wholly owned by Roger Oliver White and the E stood for enterprises. It also went on to explain that Suzanne Enterprises was part of a large restaurant operation and wholly owned by his sister, Ms. Susan Stone and the entire company was managed by a Ms. Peggy Thomas. It also went on to say it was now one of the best managed real estate companies in the three state region and had paid off almost every loan ahead of time. They had pulled off a complete and quick turnaround of the once bankrupt building that was now their headquarters and in six months had increased occupancy from a mere fifteen percent to close to ninety, and was considered miraculous by local market standards as they brought in new tenants and consolidated space. That the company assets were now valued in the billions of dollars and were continuing to grow. The fast growing company was a wholly owned family business. Roger asked when did the magazine come out, and Susan said

yesterday. Roger then said I guess we should get ready
for a knock on the front door very soon.

It wasn't even an hour after Roger made the remark,
when Maria came and informed them that their parents
were waiting in the living room and had asked to see all
of them. The three of them went downstairs and Mr. and
Mrs. White were sitting and waiting for them and they
expected the old man to be really pissed off, he wasn't as
he stood up, he had a broad grin on his face as he hugged
Roger, Susan and then Peggy, and congratulated all of
them and said he was so very proud of them all. Mr.
White said he figured one day Roger would surpass him
especially after the time he took his tuition money and
bought the building he lived in when he was in college,
said that he was impressed then and said to Susan he
knew about one of her clubs which had made him cringe,
but had no idea of the extent of her interest in these
fantastic restaurants and said he should have picked up
on it sooner with the reserved tables and the extra
attention by staff. He said he was sorry he had so under
estimated her abilities as he hugged her tightly again and
kissed her. He then turned to Peggy and said you young
lady as he looked at Peggy are a proud and wonderful
addition to the family, and said he had no clue as to her
involvement. He said I love all of you and turned back to
Roger and asked if he still wanted to be third vice
president of the White company. Roger said of course
and it would be an honor. Mr. White said to Susan your
next in line and then Peggy; we have to keep it in the
family. Roger said he would now begin donating to the
family trust now since that Peggy had lowered their debt

levels substantially and then he wouldn't have to be burdened with which donations to make and to whom. Mrs. White came and hugged and kissed him and said he was the best son any mother would ever want. Roger suggested they have a drink as they all went up the winding staircase upstairs to the terrace and Roger fixed drinks for everyone. Mr. White proposed a toast to the continued success of the ROWE Company. They were happy and Roger told his dad he thought he would be pissed off at him and Susan. Mr. White said he loved them too much and was glad that they were such a success and it made him very proud. He then asked Roger about that offer you put on the table then so quickly snatched away. Roger laughed and said there was a story behind that and would tell him one day soon as Susan stood by his side and said we thought you would be really upset, and then wondered how long it would take for you to figure out about those huge letters across the street. Roger Sr. laughed and said it did strike him as being familiar, but just couldn't place his finger on it and knew Roger owned some properties but had no idea of how many and then found out about each one of Susan's restaurants and most all of them were located in his various buildings and properties.

He said when he first read the article he wasn't sure what he had just read and had to read it again, and just to be sure he wasn't delirious, asked Anne to read it to him. That's when he said to her he had to see us immediately, and Anne thought something was seriously wrong but was surprised that Peggy was a major player and part of the business, besides actually running the company day to day. He said this was very good news and would boost his business just through association. He hugged Roger again and said you couldn't make me prouder son. It was a very happy occasion for the White family as Anne and Peggy sat and talked and Anne said they should come to the summer house for a weekend soon.

Mr. White was as happy and proud of them as he and Mrs. White returned next door and told Anne he couldn't get over what they had accomplished. He told his wife it gave him new life just knowing they would succeed. Anne said Roger was going to donate to the White charitable trust fund which would help a lot of good causes, and suggested to him that Peggy be placed on the board of the trust. Anne stated after talking with her she was very level headed and would make a very good choice and possibly assumes the chairmanship position one day because of her adept management skills. He said you are probably right about that and it couldn't be a better choice. Mr. White suggested she give her a call now. Anne picked up the phone and called and asked if Peggy would come next door. Shortly there was a knock at the door and Peggy appeared by herself and was shown into the living room as Anne greeted her again and asked her to take a seat. Ethel Anne White asked her if she would be willing to sit on the board of the White charitable trust. Peggy said she would be honored by the position and readily accepted. Anne said she was delighted and they hugged and Anne said you are the perfect woman for Roger, and that she loved her, and said if you need anything or have any questions feel free to ask. She said I am always available if you need to talk, as they walked to the front door. Peggy kissed her and returned home. When she returned she had tears in her eyes and Roger and Susan thought something was wrong until Peggy said Anne had asked her to sit on the board of the trust fund. They hugged her and Peggy said Anne hugged her and said she loved her also.

Peggy said to Roger and Susan she wanted some sex because she felt so warm inside and never felt this loved before as she hugged them both. Roger said lets have another drink because this has been a most wonderful week and you need to relax. They went to the terrace and fixed some more drinks as Peggy's emotions got the best of her as Roger and Susan had her between them on the extra-large chase lounge. Peggy said she just needed to digest it all and was glad they were here with her.

That night the three of them engaged in some passionate sex and very much enjoyed each other like they hadn't done in several weeks now that things were working more smoothly and the way they wanted their business to operate, and now they were going to enjoy themselves even more with each other once again.

Chapter Ten

The following weeks were filled with even more excitement for Peggy now as she attended her first board meeting of the White Charitable Trust and was welcomed with open arms. The chairwoman was Ethel Anne White and in attendance also was, Roger White Sr., Roger and also Susan. Also in attendance was the current vice president of the White Company and several other company and very prominent local figures. This meeting was just a formality since Ethel Anne usually was the one who decided who was going to benefit from their donations anyway. But this meeting of the board was for the introduction and nomination of Ms. Peggy Thomas, the soon to become Mrs. Peggy White and Rogers wife. It was a very short meeting as they usually were and was held in the esteemed board room of the White Company. After the meeting Roger invited his mother and father and the other members of the board on a tour the offices of ROWE, just across the street. They as a group walked across the street and across the open plaza as Roger had very much hoped they would accept his invitation and had arraigned to have a photographer take a group photo of them standing before the now large letters on the plaza. A group photo of all the women together, and then one of him and his dad, and his mother and father together and him with Susan and Peggy. Then they entered the building and went to the second floor and were given a tour as Peggy did the honors and explained what every department did, she was very proud and Roger was even more proud of her. They were shown to Rogers's expansive office and his dad said he was very impressed and could see the White Company's building across the plaza from Rogers large office windows. Shortly after Susan said she had arraigned a lunch for them all and the cars were coming around front and were waiting as they all reached the lobby and then to the circular driveway where the cars were waiting as they all departed.

Susan then took them to her newest restaurant, the Barrier Reef Sea food restaurant and it had a beautiful sea port décor and was very comfortable inside and the menu was all seafood with the exception of some dishes with chicken and steak along with sea food. Mr. Roger White Sr. enjoyed his order of shrimp and lobster, Roger and Susan ordered the broiled chicken with shrimp, and Anne and Peggy, the salmon dinners. Roger ordered two bottles of red wine and everyone enjoyed their meal. Anne said it was such a bountiful meal for lunch she might have to skip dinner. All the meals wear accompanied by a salad or coleslaw. When everyone finished Susan used her dinner's card. Mr. White asked Susan about the dinner's card and she explained how it worked, and how it included the tip. And she went on to explain that Peggy had refined the program and it was now a real bonus to their business and more people than ever were using it now and made for more repeat customers and the employees loved it also because they made money off the card besides there wages. Peggy added there was a rewards program at the end of the year for people who reached a certain level based on a monetary amount and that had increased business and caused them to expand the accounts department. It also helped keep track of inventory and cut down on a lot of undue waste. Susan said Peggy and her would make sure he received one and would make applications available to all the White Company employees. Peggy said that gave her another idea, and told Susan she would discuss it with her later.

Susan said they opened a brand new large storage building what, Peggy called an interactive warehouse where all her foods were delivered to one location, and each restaurant sent their orders in electronically and at the end of the day there orders were filled and prepared, and then shipped, and deliveries were made very early in the morning. It allowed her to buy more supplies in bulk and save even more money. Dad said he was very impressed and that the food was superb and would recommend eating here to his friends. They departed and Susan took everyone back to work. Mrs. White stayed in the limousine and headed home as Mr. White and Roger headed to the White Building, and Susan and Peggy headed back inside to ROWE headquarters. Peggy said she needed to check a few things first then her and Susan were going shopping because Susan wanted to get her a gift for her birthday since she had helped Roger.

They spent about an hour in the office before they headed to an exclusive and upscale women's clothing store where Peggy found some dresses she liked and told Susan she wanted her as they soon headed home. Once they got home it wasn't long before the two of them were in bed making love to one another and then they showered together and went and laid out on the terrace and talked. Peggy and Susan discussed making spot checks in the day time as well as night and questioned whether it was really necessary to go so often or did any real good? They decided maybe they shouldn't go as often and not to all the restaurants and clubs on the same nights and days, and make it totally random. Peggy said the Barrier Reef was a real surprise and had watched the revenues since it opened, but that was the first time eating there and the food was great. Susan said she wasn't planning on opening any more this year as they had just opened the food warehouse and was letting things shake out first before adding any more restaurants. Peggy said the idea that struck her when they were at lunch and mentioned sending club card invitations to Mr. White's employees gave her the idea of mailing out applications. Maybe start with a few select locations or better still certain companies, banks or originations. Susan said that sounds great but would like to keep the exclusivity for right now. Peggy said we will start with the White company first, and then see what happens, and Susan said ok.

It wasn't long before Roger soon appeared and fixed himself a drink and sat down and said he and dad had a good long talk. Roger said dad pointed out we should start to diversify more when we feel satisfied we have lowered our debt to a comfortable level, and should invest in some long term stocks and even treasuries. I told him we had some treasury certificates and had intended on purchasing even more on a regular quarterly basis because he said too many eggs in one basket wasn't good and we should build up a hedge fund. I told him about our hotel stocks and how it was in the plans but we hadn't reached the level I wanted us to be at quite yet. He said that he understood and would send us recommendations only when he felt we may have overlooked something. Susan said sounds like he wants us to play it safe. Roger said yes and had pointed out how fortunate we have been so far without any real serious loses and wanted us to avoid having any setbacks though he did stress that they would eventually come, but said a solid diversified portfolio would always be a good hedge against swings in the market place. He also stressed having a cash reserve and went back to the treasuries as a way to stash and benefit from the interest rates ups and downs, and another thing was a reserve of precious metals and having the actual metal in our possession. I told him we would discuss some of our next moves with him and put a plan in action as soon as I had discussed it first with both of you. He said he was very happy with my business associates and said we made a great team and to keep it up.

Susan said that's why I love him; he has always been straight with me or rather us. Roger said mom has also and as a matter of fact; we have been lucky to have such good parents that really love us and now Peggy. Roger said you two look very relaxed. Peggy said she and Susan made love and now she felt so much better. Roger said I am happy about that baby, we all have each other and that's what so good about us. Susan said her and Peggy were discussing her pop up checks and was going to change how they did them and wondered if you wanted to participate. He said sure it's our combined business and said as a matter of fact we should all receive the same amount of pay as a matter of fairness. Susan said she agreed with that and then we can invest what we don't really need. Susan said a million dollars each a year in salary should be sufficient. Roger said he agreed and will take care of that tomorrow and institute a new investment fund with equal participation between the three of us. They sat and talked some more and Roger asked Peggy what kind of wedding did she want. She said the simpler the better, nothing fancy or extravagant, just a simple private affair was all she wanted since she was already here. Roger said then you pick a date and what about a honeymoon. She said the same applied to it also, something simple and nothing out of the country, with the exception of maybe Canada. Roger asked her where do you want to go then, Peggy said she would have to think about that a little longer, but a month from now would give you or rather us time to make the arrangements. He said fine and would work on it this week with her. They decided to call it a day and went inside and to bed with each other. Roger was in the middle as both women cuddled up next to him as he soon fell asleep.

Chapter Eleven

The following day after everyone had breakfast and dressed, they all rode to the office together. Roger stepped out and headed to his old office at the White Company as Susan and Peggy headed to the new food distribution warehouse to inspect the newly instituted operations. Peggy had been there several times as the warehouse was placed in full operational mode and making sure it started up and ran the way she wanted, making sure it functioned as it should and was one of the reasons why she was so very tired and went to bed early and slept most weekends. Susan had only been here twice before today as they stood to one side, out of the way and observed the pace of the operation as the employees went about performing their assigned task. Peggy questioned the managing supervisor as he escorted them around and asked if he had any suggestions or if there were any items they needed more of. And he said that so far he had made some minor adjustments with their suppliers and had observed there were certain food items he needed to have more of to cover weekend demands and pointed out some of the restaurants used more of certain items than others and said that was to be expected especially with the addition of the new sea food restaurant and the expected and the planned expansion of some of the others. Said he had increased several of the sea foods orders, and several of the frozen vegetables. Peggy said if you suspect something is out of order don't hesitate to let me know. He said for sure, and went on to say he liked the way she had organized the operation and loved the computerized ordering system for the various restaurants and thought it was also great having the backup generators for the building freezers and security systems to prevent spoilage in case of a major power outage. That along with the dry supplies, and with the kitchen supply department being located here really cut down on having to make extra deliveries for instance for just washroom, kitchen and cleaning supplies most of the time, and could have it all on one truck. He also said he had received thanks from several of the different restaurant managers because everything they needed made it on the first delivery of the day and really helped them in operating smoothly. Susan and Peggy felt they had seen enough, thanked him and went back to the office as Susan checked on her staff and Peggy went and checked the computerized files like she did every day. Susan returned and they decided to go across the street and check on Roger.

They found Roger and Mr. White ending a conference with the staff and told them it was lunch time and they were going to the Town and Country which was on the other side of the park. They called for their limousine and went to lunch as Roger Sr. said this was a completely new experience for him. Susan said it was part of her and Peggy's new approach of spot checking all of her locations randomly and she didn't call ahead, this way staff and management would never know when she might pop up, and said we have to keep them on their toes. They arrived and were shown to the reserved seating as menus were presented promptly, as they glanced over the wide selection. The waiter returned with glasses of water and asked if they were ready to place their orders. The Town and Country had a wide variety to select from for their lunch menu, from sandwiches and light meals, all with salads, to complete dinners. Roger Sr. ordered a corn beef sandwich on rye, Roger a chicken sandwich, Susan a ham sandwich and Peggy the chicken salad. It didn't take long for their food to arrive and it was delicious. The manager approached their table and asked if everyone was satisfied and they said yes as he continued walking around and checking with many of the other patrons. When they finished Peggy used her club card, and it was soon handed back with the customary receipt. They departed and returned to the office as Peggy and Susan said the staff and service were great, and we can check them off for this week, and had a board with the various locations on it and would keep track of their visits. The rest of the day was uneventful as Peggy and Susan returned home early, sat and talked with Anne for a long while and Peggy said she had told Roger she wanted a simple private ceremony and asked if she had any suggestions. Anne said a simple church ceremony was fine and made sense. They could have it at the small Protestant church down the street and Roger and her should go talk to the clergy there and set a date. Susan said she would tell him today. Anne said she would look forward to their marriage and hoped one day they have children, and said I guess you know that. Peggy said she knew and Roger had said as much the same thing but she wanted to wait a little longer. Anne said the sooner the better because you don't want to be too old because it begins to get much harder, and besides you want to be able to watch them grow up and have conversations like we are having now. Anne told her you follow your own mind sweetie, and do what you think is best for you, I have been where you are now, and it was such a wonderful experience. They spent several hours with Anne before going home as she thanked them for coming by and said don't be strangers.

Peggy and Susan returned next door and Peggy said she was going to shower before dinner and Susan said she would also as they went to their separate bedrooms. Roger was later than usual when he came home and they were ready to eat, so he washed his hands and they ate together and Peggy told him what Anne had said about the church. He said he would look into it before the week was over. He said he enjoyed lunch earlier and was late because he was looking at some market reports and said he had set up an account for them at a local bank and had made their first deposit. It amounted to three million dollars into a three year certificate of deposit at a guaranteed six percent interest and it was the first of such deposits he would begin hopefully making every six months and into various funds. He said he checked all of their investments, and the treasuries, the gains were about average. He said he was very tired and would relax tonight and get some needed rest. They ate and when they finished Susan and Peggy wet upstairs on the terrace and relaxed and looked at some fashion magazines and talked. Roger came up briefly, had a drink and kissed both and said good night and departed. Peggy asked about the bedrooms up here and Susan said it's very nice but Roger had decided to stay downstairs. Peggy said she liked the bedrooms up here because it was so much more open and much larger than downstairs and said there are two and why don't we move up here. There was an extra-large living room and the bedrooms were so much larger and had room sized walk-in closets and the bathrooms were very elegant and much larger. Susan said maybe you're right, maybe it's time for a change. Peggy said she would change the colors and the children could have the bedrooms downstairs. Susan said don't tell me you changed your mind, or are you pregnant. Peggy said no she wasn't, but just wanted to stay ahead of the curve, and said she didn't intend to stop working if she had children with all the help they had at home. Said her schedule provided her with enough time to raise children and anyways it wasn't going to happen too soon and not until Roger was ready also, and then I will always have you to help, Auntie Susan. Susan came over and she and Peggy hugged one another and Susan said she wanted to sleep with her again tonight as they went and fixed another drink and talked more about the future. After a while they went to Peggy's bedroom where they undressed and fell asleep together.

The following morning on their way to work they stopped as Roger and Peggy went inside the local church a couple blocks from their residence and talked to the pastor. They discussed having a small wedding and he asked when, as he looked in his appointment book, Roger turned and looked at Peggy, she said in three weeks and on a Saturday. He looked at them both, and Peggy said, around two pm would be fine. The pastor said a small donation would cover the cost and Roger made out a check for five thousand dollars and handed it to him, the pastor wrote down their information, and looked up and said done, and thank you. Susan was waiting outside in the car as they came out smiling and told Susan the date and she made a note of it and told them she would handle the reception and reassured Peggy it would be a small private affair. Roger said they would get the license sometime today around noon and asked Peggy, would around one would be ok with you. She replied yes it would. They continued on their way to work and Roger went to his new office and his dad said that he didn't have to come in every day since he had his own business to run and fully understood. After lunch Roger and Peggy went to city hall to get their marriage license and soon returned to work around three, and found Susan and since it was Friday, decided to go home early, but first walked across the street and went to his dad's office, and showed him the license. Roger Sr. hugged him and Peggy as they said they were calling it a day as he checked with his secretary and said he was leaving shortly also as they waited for him and they all left together.

When they arrived home and had gone to their apartment Maria informed them Mrs. White had called and invited them all to dinner at six thirty. Susan said then we have time to shower and change as everyone went to their bedrooms to clean up. Peggy told Roger she wanted them to move upstairs after he had the rooms painted a different color, he said of course, and said see you shortly. It wasn't long before they were all ready to go next door. Susan and Peggy were dressed casually and Roger had on some shorts and a t-shirt. They were greeted by Martha the Whites maid and housekeeper, as they went inside and Anne greeted them and said she wanted to have a casual family dinner with them all. Mr. White was washing up and greeted the group as he came into the large living room. Roger said he and Peggy had made the arrangements at the church and had gotten their license. The meal was served by Martha and Frida there cook. It was a beautiful meal of roasted chicken, rice and vegetables and very tasty. Roger and Susan had grown up on Frida's cooking and always very much enjoyed it. Peggy complimented the cook and said she really enjoyed the meal and now knew why Roger grew up so to be so strong and hansom. Frida thanked her as she started clearing the table with Martha and then dessert was served. They ate and enjoyed their food and afterwards Anne suggested they go to the living room for a bit. They talked a while and Roger gave his mom the date for their marriage at the church and thanked her for the church information. Anne said she was glad they had picked a date and looked forward to the occasion. Roger Sr. Proposed a toast before Roger, Peggy and Susan departed to their home next door. Roger Sr. toasted to long life and prosperity. They all hugged one another before leaving and saying good bye.

When Peggy, Roger and Susan returned home they went upstairs and Peggy showed him the bedroom she wanted for them and told him the color she wanted and also wanted Susan to move into the bedroom just across the hall and large stair case. The rooms were so much larger and had walk-in closets and huge bathrooms and told him the children could occupy the ones downstairs. Roger looked at her surprised and asked if she was pregnant, to which she responded, no not yet but was planning for the future and said she wasn't giving up working before, or after child birth, that she may take some maternity leave but still wanted to have a career. He looked at her and smiled, and said whatever you want to do was fine with him. She also told him she wanted Susan up here with us, which her love was for him and her and saw no need for a change in the way they were living. Roger said he agreed with her and wanted her happy and asked if she needed a color chart for the color changes. She said it would be very helpful and he called downstairs to the building superintendent's office and asked for a color chart to be brought up so she could pick the colors and he would leave instructions later. The super said ok and he would have the chart brought up right away.

Roger fixed them some drinks and they toasted to a bright future. A half hour later Rose brought them the color charts. Peggy looked through it and went and walked around the expansive space and chose two colors, then went to the bathroom and decided on a brighter white for it. Then with Susan, went to her new bedroom and chose a new color also and agreed with Peggy on a brighter bathroom color with one wall a warm blue. Roger wrote down the color changes and said he would give them to the super Monday in case they decided to make any changes.

Peggy said she wanted to sleep with them both as they went downstairs, and Roger said she was right about upstairs with the larger open living room and more privacy. Susan said she was now looking forward to the move. Roger said we will have more room if someone visits or spends the night. They went to Rogers's bedroom and they all undressed and Susan said you know I haven't heard any bells lately, and Roger said you know you are right as he slipped on his robe and went to check on Min. He found her sleeping and woke her up, she opened her eyes and Roger told her to stand and remove the night shirt she was wearing. The rings were still in place in her nipples as he checked for any infections, then had her lay and spread her legs open as he checked her labia and found nothing wrong and the bells were still where they should be. He told her to stand and bend over as he smacked her ass a few times before he turned and left. He returned and said her rings and bells were in place and she was sleeping. Susan asked Peggy, do you want her, and she said no, not tonight. Roger climbed in bed between the two highly sexed women as they pounced on him. Peggy sat on him as he began getting quickly aroused as Susan sat on his face, they kissed, as he licked Susan and Peggy rode him, and then they switched places, then both got off and licked him until he climaxed, then the two women kissed each other and Peggy laid on her back and Roger got down between her legs and licked and sucked her until she climaxed again as Susan felt her breast and kissed her, then Susan laid on her back and Peggy was between her thighs as Roger kissed and felt on her as Peggy brought her to a rousing climax and then the three laid next to one another with Susan in the middle as they hugged and kissed, an a short time later they moved there sex play to the shower where they continued to feel, and touch, and bring one another to rousing climaxes again before bathing one another.

When they left the shower all three were fully satisfied as they oiled and applied lotion before putting on wraps and robes and going back upstairs to the terrace for some drinks.

Peggy said she liked it up here and wouldn't have to go far after the move upstairs. Roger said she was right and didn't know why he hadn't moved up here before now, and said as soon as its painted, and told Peggy and Susan to leave the furniture downstairs and just buy it new for the large empty rooms and told Peggy since you will be my wife you should have the privilege of choosing the furnishings, but asked her not to make it to girlie. She said don't worry it won't be that way. They had their drinks and soon went back downstairs to Rogers's bedroom and crawled in under the sheets together for a well deserved rest.

Chapter Twelve

That next morning while having another wonderful breakfast, Roger suggested they all go together and pick out some of the furniture for upstairs and especially the new bedroom sets and spend the day shopping together since they had never done it before. Then he and Peggy could agree on the new furnishings. Peggy said that sounds so wonderful and Susan said it should be loads of fun. So everyone agreed and it was settled then, and soon they finished eating breakfast. Roger left to get ready and would meet them in the living room and said, he would call down for the building super to come up and would show him what walls to paint what color and if any of you are finished dressing when he's here come up to make sure I have the work or painting you want done correct. They both said ok as he left the dining room table and went to his bedroom. After he had dressed Roger called downstairs to the building superintendent's office and asked if he could come up so he could show him what work he wanted done. Fifteen minutes later there was a knock at the front door, it was the assistant superintendent and Roger greeted him as they shook hands and then went upstairs and Roger handed him the color chart and showed him what he wanted done. Roger asked for the bright white for both bath rooms and the one wall in Susan's bathroom to be painted blue above the tile and showed him the color she had chosen as he made notes in his small note book. Just then Peggy appeared and shortly after Susan as they took over from Roger and they showed him what colors and on which walls. The assistant super made sure he had everything correct and then verified it. He then asked Mr. White when he wanted it painted. Roger said as soon as possible, since he knew they also had other jobs around the building, but had a full time painter on staff. The assistant super said as soon as they had the paint they would start the job right away. Roger thanked him as he departed.

Susan and Peggy said they were ready for their shopping adventure with him as Roger pulled out his cell phone and called for the family limousine and informed the driver he would be with them all day. They went downstairs and soon departed. When they left the lobby Roger told the driver where to take them first. They went to one the best furniture stores in the city because they had the widest selection of furniture and more than half the apartments, condos and lofts were furnished with furniture from there stores wide selection. They stepped out in front of the store and quickly entered as they went directly to the bedroom sets department. Peggy soon found the bed set she wanted, it was an oversized king size bed called a California king and Susan said she would get one also but wanted a slightly different style and finish. Peggy said with the closet being already furnished they didn't need any dressers and they then went to the living room section and looked over the extremely wide selection of furniture. Peggy soon chose a comfortable double couch set and chair combination for the bed room. Then she and Susan chose a living room set with two different large size couches and chairs to match, and since the room was so large they purchased two sets. Susan picked for her bed room a similar lounging set, but the materials and finishes were slightly different. A salesman wrote down there orders for all they had chosen and Peggy said she wanted a nice low cabinet and found just the one she wanted for the bed room to go with the other furnishings. Peggy said that's a start and the rest she figured they would add over time after moving into the new bedroom.

Susan said she couldn't wait to roll around in the large bed with them both. The same salesman accompanied them for all their various selections. Peggy picked some lamps and several large Persian rugs for the living room since it had a hard wood floor. The bedrooms had wall to wall carpet and said she was satisfied with the texture and color. They had spent half a day in the one store and it was past lunch time and both Susan and Peggy said they were finished and famished. When Peggy had chosen something she would ask Roger if he was happy with her selection and he said he was, and commented that she had very good taste. Susan soon asked the question, where, should we go for lunch, as Roger called for the limo, and Peggy said how about the Passion Fruit. Susan said what a good choice since we haven't been there in quite a while. They exited the store as their car was waiting, and informed the driver of their next destination and were soon headed for the Passion Fruit. It took almost an hour since it was a really nice day and people were about and traffic was unusually heavy. They finally arrived and there was a small line as they walked inside and the maître recognized Susan and Peggy and showed them to their reserved table. A waiter soon appeared considering the restaurant was filled to capacity and Susan's table was the only one available. The manager had been informed by the maître that Susan and Peggy along with Roger were here and breathed a sigh of relief that her table hadn't been taken by mistake.

They studied the menu and Roger ordered the chicken salad, Peggy the chicken wing lunch, and Susan the broiled steak burger. Peggy made a note on her phone to be placed on their bulletin board Monday when they went to the office. The Passion Fruit was a really very upscale sports bar, with large digital television screens hanging from the ceiling with great viewing angles from every seat and booth and with all the various sports channels on, and had been one of their most popular restaurants and was one of the leaders in gross revenue especially during play offs and different sports finals. Peggy said to Susan maybe we should look to expand this into a chain of restaurants after we feel we have a handle on things and expand further outside of the city limits. Susan looked at her and said that might work. Peggy said she didn't want to make it a stock company because she felt the quality went down in the drive to make money, but would be more open to franchise restaurants with company owned in between as the real drivers and leaders of the brand, giving it real net worth. Susan said we will have to talk more about this later as their food soon arrived. Roger said the food was delicious and Peggy said the chicken wings were cooked really well, as Susan enjoyed the burger and fries. When they finished they were very satisfied with the meal and the service as the waiter presented the bill. Peggy handed him her card and he soon returned with the card and a receipt, then they prepared to leave. On the ride home Susan said that was a first at that restaurant at this time of day and on a Saturday at that. Peggy said that was the best pop up ever because they were operating at their peak, and performed well and were doing very good. Said she rated the service as excellent, and now she understood how the critics made their choices.

Roger asked if Susan had any shows going on at any of her clubs. Susan said just some bands at Town and Country and nothing much at Whips and Chains but whip Master Ron would be on at eight pm and other than that there really wasn't much happening this weekend. Susan asked him what was on his mind, what did he want to do this evening for entertainment. He asked her about the whip master. Said he was one of the local masters and a regular club member; Master Ron was going to demonstrate on several of his slaves some whipping techniques. Roger said he would like to go since he didn't want to attend any shows or movies and it had been a while since feeding his kinky side, asking Peggy if she wanted to attend. She said sure and they all decided to go after stopping briefly at home.

That afternoon after a short rest and a change of clothes, the three of them headed to Whips and Chains for the floor show with whip master Ron. There was a small mixed crowd of both men and women, but tonight seemed to be more women in attendance than men. Many members were women and dominatrix and sometimes also performed and several had put on some really fantastic shows. As always in the exclusive private club the three of them sat in Susan's elevated private booth in the rear with a full view of the stage and all the tables with its variety of club patrons. Peggy sat in the middle, between Susan and Roger as whip Master Ron came on stage, taking a bow to a rousing applause, then turned and led his first female subject out, an onto the stage to another rousing applause as some dramatic music played in the background. This was Peggy's first time at Whips and Chains, and both Roger and Susan noticed she was beginning to get very excited as Master Ron proceeded to cuff the woman; she had a collar on as the master removed her loose fitting sheer robe as she now stood completely nude and bare foot before the excited audience. He attached the cuffs to her wrist before he raised her arms up above her head, attaching them as they were spread far apart to the wide metal bar above her head, then attached cuffs to her slender ankles before attaching a rope to one ankle and raising it up behind her and attaching it to the same end of the bar that one of her arms was attached to. Now she was standing only on one leg, as her vagina was fully exposed to the now excited audience. Then he pulled out a blindfold and covered her eyes. The master then retrieved a length of bamboo about a yard long; the ends had been splintered into several long thin strands and covered half the length. Then he began passing it over the helpless woman's body as she hung exposed, she flinched as he passed it all across the sensitive parts of her body. Then with a quick motion he struck her thigh on the one leg she was standing on, as he then gently rubbed it against her thighs and between her legs and up the leg that was attached to the rope. The master released her leg from above her head and retrieved some thin strips of bamboo similar to thin chopsticks with rubber bands attached at the ends. He removed the rubber bands from one end and placed the woman's ample areola between the sticks and reattaching the rubber bands to the loose end squeezing her areola and nipples between the thin sticks causing them to bulged out, then did the other breast, as she now stood with her breast clamped as the master attached a spreader bar to the woman's ankles spreading her legs as far apart as possible, she stood now fully exposed to the audience as they clapped and cheered.

Master Ron now took a bow, and returned with a cat-o-nine tails or leather flogger and rubbed the whip all over her body lightly before he began whipping her, watching her jerk as he struck her several times as she began to moan. He retrieved some clamps that he attached to her now very swollen nipples and knelt down and attached the others to her labia, before he retrieved a wide leather belt. He turned her around so the audience would see her anus, as he then proceeded after he doubled up the leather strap, to strike each ass cheek ten times, and alternating as her ass started to turn crimson. He turned her back around and reached for a smaller whip and whipped her now swollen breast. He removed the clamps and the bamboo strips he used to squeeze her breast as they became even more sensitive as he cruelly pinched them as she cringed and her knees bent. He went and returned with some small heavy weights and attached them to the clamps on her labia as they stretched her lips down as she moaned. Then pinched her nipples and twisted them before removing the vaginal clamps. He now returned with a wide leather strap, then proceeded to whip the woman all over as she jerked from the strikes, he spared no part of her outstretched body, before he then whipped her between her spread legs from in front and then from behind until she climaxed and jerked uncontrollably as he then proceeded to hold a hand held vibrator to her clit as she screamed loudly. She climaxed continuously then hung limp after fainting, as the audience applauded for several minutes. He released her legs from the spreader bar and stood her up and removed the blind fold as he slapped her face as she came to before he released her arms, as he held her before collapsing onto the floor, before he carried her to the side of the stage and placed her in a wooden chair and cuffing her arms behind the chair back.

Master Ron returned and took a bow to a rousing ovation before he led another willing woman onto the stage, she was slender and wore only cuffs on her arms and legs and a large waist belt as the master rolled out a low table as he directed her to lay on it, with her back on the table the master attached a bar to her wrist and one to her ankles and attached her raised arms to another bar overhead then her legs, and finally the waist belt. When he finished, he went to the side and turned a crank as the woman was raised above the table to about chest height of the master, as he pushed the table aside and then rotated the woman around for all the audience to see. Then he used a whip with three lengths of narrow leather on her suspended body as she jerked and he left whelps on her. Then he inserted into her a vibrator as she jerked violently as he continued to whip her and only stopped when she climaxed and fainted as her head hung down and he rolled the table back over and lowered her and released her bonds. After releasing her, he poured ice cold water on her face as she came around and then made her climb off the table and stand. Then he attached her arms above her head as she had a look of real fear on her face. The master then brought the first woman back on stage and attached her arms above her head also so the two slaves were hanging for all to see.

Master Ron inserted into both women small vibrators and tied both women's legs together at the knees and stood back as they moaned and jerked after he turned them on before he picked up a whip and struck both as they jerked from the whipping and the sensations from the vibrators as he turned them around so the audience could see the marks as he spared no portion of their beautiful naked bodies, as both climaxed continually. When he stopped both were in tears and he asked them what do you say, and they both replied in weak voices thank you Master Ron, as he made them repeat it louder for all to hear before he slowly released them to a rousing standing applause from the audience.

Afterwards Roger said he didn't expect to see a show like that, but said it was very entertaining and had gotten him very excited, as he looked at Peggy and Susan. Susan whispered to Peggy that she needed some sex now, and asked Roger to call for the limousine; it was time for them to go now. He called and said the limo was waiting as they left the club and told Susan they were going to the penthouse before releasing the driver for the night. They headed upstairs to the penthouse, it had been a couple months since they all were here last but sent a maid once a week to clean up and dust. Susan said she was very horny and needed some sex and Peggy said she felt the same and both wanted Roger to tie them up and play with them as they headed for the play room. Peggy and Susan helped each other undress and putting on wrist and ankle cuffs. When they finished Roger hung both women from the long metal bar above their heads and then told them they were his bitches and needed to be punished. He felt between both women's legs and both were dripping wet as he touched them. Peggy and Susan both climaxed right away and it didn't take either very long before vaginal fluids ran down their thighs. Roger felt freaky and knelt between Peggy legs and felt her freshly shaven vagina and licked her as she was highly aroused and inserted several fingers inside her as she jerked with a another violent climax and continued to feel her as he stood and kissed her and said your ass is next when I return. He next went over to Susan and bit her neck, kneeling down to her very wet shaven vagina licking it slowly and fingering her just as he had did with Peggy, he licked and sucked her now extended clit as she climaxed and he continued to lick and suck her, before standing and kissing her and feeling her as she climaxed again. He stood before the two women and said you bitches need to feel the whip. He went to a cabinet and returned with a whip, with several long braided strands, as Susan begged please no master as he brought it down across her breast working it across both women's body as it stung the soft smooth flesh and left small red lines on their out stretched hanging bodies, after about twenty lashes each he stopped and returned to the cabinet and returned with a clamp and attached one ankle of each woman together. When he stood back and looked at their legs, it formed the letter M. Peggy and Susan were highly excited and frightened at the same time since Roger had really been the passive one up to now and was seldom aggressive. Susan had always been the aggressive one before now. Roger was beginning to enjoy being a dominant. Roger removed some clamps and attached them to their now swollen nipples and labia's. He returned with some lubricant and liberally lubed each woman's anus, then returned with two large butt plugs which he slowly inserted into each. Roger stood before his sister Susan and asked her who she belonged to as he played with her as the clamps hung from her vaginal lips as the excitement rose and became even more highly excited and frightened as Roger flicked at her clit. She replied you master, always you as she exploded with a violent climax like none she ever had before, as he kissed and tonged her and told her he was going to fuck the shit out of her slut ass.

He stood before a trembling and now very highly aroused and frightened Peggy, he said to her you are my bitch now also, nibbling at her neck as he felt between her legs and played with her wet pussy and flicked her clit with his finger as he talked dirty and demeaning to her and said she was his slave bitch as she climaxed and jerked violently. Roger said time for you two bitchs to serve as he released the cuff holding together their legs and told the two weak in the knees women to stand up or he would whip them more. He removed the clamps from them both as they hung there and he left the room as they begged for him to return. Roger came back a short time later after taking a pee and released Peggy and cuffed her hands behind her back, then Susan and did the same and ordered them to the bedroom and told them to kneel in the bed with their heads down and asses up. They still had the butt plugs inserted in there asses as he had the wide semi soft leather paddle with him as he began spanking both women and ordering them to spread their legs far apart which they did. Then he climbed behind Peggy and plunged himself into her hot wet pussy as she climaxed again, then moved over and did the same to Susan and after she climaxed he laid between the two and ordered them to suck him off as they licked and sucked him he told them they were his dirty bitches and better do as they were told or he would punish them even more. Shortly after he came and made them lick him clean, he then made them lay next to him. Their hands were still cuffed behind them and the butt plugs were still inside of them both. He asked them who he was as they both replied he was their master. He felt them and told them to roll and bend over as he removed the anal plugs and went to the bathroom. When he returned he had a couple pieces of rope. He cuffed their hands in front of them as he had them lay on their backs and tied their hand above their heads, tying their hands to the head of the bed. He cuffed them together at the ankle again as he climbed between Peggy's legs and licked her wet pussy and licked and played with her clit until she came again, then he did Susan the same way and soon she climaxed also. The two women were now totally exhausted. He waited before untying them and removing the cuffs and ordered them to stand as he hugged them and said he loved them as they kissed him passionately. They all went to the shower where he had them kneel and gave them both a golden shower, then turned the water on and they all bathed. When they finished and dried off and had oiled themselves they went and had drinks and sat on the terrace, taking in the view of the city at night. Peggy and Susan sat holding hands as Roger stood taking in the view before sitting down with them. Susan asked him just what happened to him tonight and said you never were this aggressive before. He said he couldn't explain it, but said the whip masters Ron's show had turned him on and he just felt like that. Susan said she enjoyed it and Peggy said she did also and loved him and would always be here for him. Roger knelt down and thanked them for being in his life and allowing him to be free with his feelings and said he loved them. He asked if they wanted another drink and they said yes as he went to fix another, Susan and Peggy kissed and felt on one another under their robes, and getting aroused again.

Roger returned with their drinks and Susan said when they finished she wanted more sex with them both. They finished and went inside to the bedroom and continued having sex until they all fell asleep very exhausted.

Chapter Thirteen

The following morning they woke, and Peggy was the first one out of bed as she went and washed up, then returned before Roger and Susan decided to get up and returned to bed and kissed Roger, and told him she loved him and was his forever. Peggy said as they lay in bed she would fix breakfast as Roger and Susan finally crawled out of bed and headed for the bathroom. Soon they were all headed for the kitchen as Roger made the coffee and Susan began helping Peggy. It wasn't long before they were sitting down eating, and Peggy commented on how satisfying the sex was with the two of them and knew she would be very happy now and couldn't wait for them to move upstairs at home. Roger suggested they should relax today and maybe plan and discuss the restaurant franchises before taking it outside of the local market with several new locations and before they jumped into the multi state market. Peggy said that sounds like a winner and they should look at some of the newly gentrified neighborhoods as a starting point. He said he had a few places as possible locations now but suggested they really try and relax more today since the past several months have been very hectic. When they finished eating they cleaned up and washed their dishes and Roger grabbed Peggy and kissed her and then turned around and grabbed Susan and kissed her also and said he was so very happy and very satisfied with his life and with both of them in it as they all hugged. They decided to dress and go home and since it was just seven blocks away and on the same side of the park as Sutton Place, decided to walk home. Susan said by the time they got home it would be lunch time anyways. Susan said after last night she would be overdue for some more food by then.

Roger said let's look around the corner of the next block since they were walking and their might be a potentially new location since it was basically a residential neighborhood and might present them with a really good opportunity. After they had dressed and went downstairs they walked around the corner and there stood a twenty story building with a large vacant space on the ground floor which had been a restaurant several months before but had closed and was now out of business. The building was an office building and Roger wrote down the address and the management company's name as they peered into the vacant space and Susan said she didn't really care for the location and said she would rather explore more open locations farther out from the central city as they turned around and headed for home. After about an hour's walk they arrived home, and went upstairs and began to relax. Roger asked Maria to fix them a light lunch.

Roger took a hot shower and returned wearing shorts and a t-shirt. Peggy and Susan went and bathed also and they all met up at the dining room table for the light lunch of tuna salad on lettuce with crackers. When they finished they went their separate ways with Peggy and Susan sitting on the terrace as Roger went to the study to review some information from the daily newspapers he had collected all week and several other publications.

Peggy said to Susan, she didn't know what was wrong with her but wanted to have more sex after thinking about yesterday and especially last evening, asking if she would now take her. Susan stood and took her by the hand and they went to her bedroom and closed the door to undress and Peggy asked Susan to please spank her as she knelt with her head down in Susan's bed with her legs spread apart and asked Susan to please use a belt on her. Susan pulled out a leather belt and rolled it up after undressing and kissed Peggy's upturned ass before she began spanking Peggy's ass, starting out whipping her lightly at first then gradually harder as Peggy played with her overly excited and very hot pussy. Susan told her to move her hand as she whipped between her legs then told her to turn over and to grab her ankles as she lay on her back and very exposed to Susan. Susan whipped her pussy and clitoris until she climaxed, then Susan knelt down and licked her causing her to have several more climaxes and sticking her fingers inside of Peggy as she lay panting. Susan rubbed her buttocks as Peggy moaned and told her move further up in the bed as Susan climbed on top of her and pressed her hot vagina into Peggy's face as she licked Susan's vagina. Susan fingered and played with Peggy's very hot wet pussy causing her to climax again as Susan came to a rousing climax also, as Peggy continued to lick Susan vagina and then her ass. They both climaxed as they rolled over with Peggy on top as they continued eating one another and after both had climaxed several times fell to each other's side panting and very out of breath. Susan sat up and turned around and held Peggy as they continued to feel on each other and continuing to climax again as they kissed. They finally made their way to the bathroom where they urinated on one another kissing more saying they were truly sisters as they turned the water on and bathed each other feeling and climaxing over and over again as they fingered each other ass and vaginas until they were fully exhausted. When they finished they went and oiled their bodies and climbed into bed holding one another and they both soon fell sound asleep.

Roger after looking at some possible new locations sat in his recliner reading and soon dosed off into a deep sleep and when he woke it was late in the evening. He went to wash his face, and to find the two loves in his life, soon finding them sleeping in Susan's bed and holding one another, he decided not to wake them. The room smelled of sex as he departed and went and fixed himself some soup. Rosé had fixed dinner and had left it in the refrigerator with a note. Rose was finished for the day and Roger would wait on Peggy and Susan to wake and eat with them later. He knew they were probably still very excited from yesterday's show and escapades afterwards since it had been quite a while since they all had sex together. Roger went to the terrace and fixed himself a drink and sat back and relaxed as he looked at the city skyline across the park as the sun was starting to set behind the buildings on the west side of the park and thought about how fortunate he was to have been born into a prosperous family, and having a step sister who he always truly loved and now soon a wife to be who shared his sexual fantasies and loved his sister as well and understood their very close and special relationship. He sipped his drink and about an hour later went and checked on his two loves. They were just beginning to wake up from their sexual exploits when they saw him enter the bedroom. Susan sat up and got out of bed and he looked at her beautiful nude body as she came and hugged him as Peggy sat up and crawled across the bed and she came over and she hugged him as well as he felt her. He said, time to feed your beautiful bodies ladies and said he would start warming the food Rose had prepared. He said he had to leave because looking at them nude was more than he could take right now and needed all his energy after last evening. Roger turned and quickly left the room and went to the kitchen to begin warming the food, setting the table and sat in the kitchen as he slowly sipped his drink.

It wasn't long before the roasted chicken with rice dish was warm enough and he set the mixed salad on the table with a couple of different salad dressings. He started dishing up the chicken and rice as Peggy and Susan came to the dining room table and sat down, and soon they were all eating together again. Susan and Peggy ate like they hadn't eaten in a week as Roger observed them and knew why they were so famished. Both went back for seconds and returned and they ate all that remained of the food. Roger cleared the table and washed the dishes as Susan and Peggy finished eating and brought him their plates as he finished washing everything. He looked at the two of them and asked if they wanted any dessert. They said no not now, as they all went back upstairs and sat on the terrace as he fixed himself another drink and sat back and relaxed. He looked at the two of them and smiled and they asked why he was smiling. Said he was thinking how lucky he was to be with the two smartest, most successful and beautiful and the sexiest women in the world, and they loved him, and said that thought would bring a smile to any man's face.

They sat and talked and massaged each other, and drank until they decided to turn in and prepare for the busy week ahead.

Chapter Fourteen

The following week Peggy was making out the list of invited guest for her marriage to Roger, it wasn't a very long list since most of her life she only made friends on occasions so the number was less than twenty, and Rogers list contained almost about the same number as he was even more of a loaner, and his best and closest friend through life and lover had always been Susan. Mr. and Mrs. Whites list of guest was slightly longer as was Peggy's parents Bob and Sarah Thomas. The small church would almost be filled to capacity. Susan handled sending out the invitations and made all the arrangements and had assigned each of her small personal staff with an appointed duty. It didn't take Susan long to have the invitations sent out and when the RSVP invites were returned she had her staff adjust the banquet hall and menu to the specific needs. Susan planned and would hold the reception at the Town and Country. The restaurant didn't open until five pm and would hardly be busy at that time of the day anyway since it was more the place for the older set that attended much later in the evening for dinner usually after seven with dancing and musicians following a night out usually at the many theaters, shows and concerts around the city's very prominent theater district and other entertainment venues downtown.

Peggy and Susan were totally surprised when Roger came and abruptly announced a change of management at the top of the ROWE Company. He said his new title would be chairman of the board and his work schedule would reflect his position and Peggy was to assume the position of CFO and Susan CEO. He stated that nothing basically would change but the titles and better suited the positions they held and duties they performed and this would allow him to better fulfill his upcoming position as one of the vice presidents at the White Company when one of the current vice presidents would soon retire. He said he sent a memo to all departments notifying them of the change and maintenance would be changing the signs in the hallways later on today. He asked them to pick an employee to fill the position of executive director or should the position be abolished. Susan said abolished since nothing changed but titles. Peggy said she agreed with her for now. Roger suggested they should pick and prepare someone to fill the several lead positions in the different departments as they planned their coming expansions. Roger said that title would be eliminated and they would revue operations every quarter then see if the position would really be needed. Both Peggy and Susan agreed that they should start grooming replacements to handle operations in their absence, and it would be prudent to do so since the company was on such a fast tracked expansion. Roger agreed and said they should start right away choosing their seconds, and each should present a list of candidates who they would revue together and be acceptable to all of us. He said it was a priority because of their rapid growth.

Susan and Peggy had been going shopping more often now during the weeks leading up to the wedding and Peggy soon found a sheik but elegant wedding dress in white that was just above the knee in front with a hem that was cut on an angle and ended just below the calf of her leg in the rear and had a small simple matching head piece with a veil. Roger didn't have to shop since he already had a tuxedo in his closet and just needed to send it out for a cleaning.

Even though it was going to be a small private wedding, it was still mentioned in the gossip columns of all the local newspapers because of their social standing in the community. Little did anyone suspect that there was one person who despised Peggy and Roger both and would surely do anything he could to hurt them. He had watched them from afar ever since that day she resigned her position at Harbor and Associates, and it wasn't long before his poor management skills came into question after her departure, and especially after several other very highly skilled and underpaid employees resigned to work at the new ROWE company. He was slowly plotting his revenge. In his sick demented mind, blamed a life time of personal failures on Peggy and would do anything to hurt her, bodily harm or even murder. She was the center of his sick and demented attention ever since Peggy had gone to upper management about his sexual harassment of her. This soon resulted in a reprimand as he was placed on probation, but not removed; as a matter of fact he had been given more responsibility to oversee the entire department after another manager in the same department resigned to raise a family after marrying a leading executive in the same company. The company logic behind this was with the increased responsibility and would have more people to supervise and hopefully would be too busy to harass her or any one person. He stopped harassing her directly, but gave her the hardest and most difficult, challenging, and important assignments which only served to sharpened her already most adept skills, and later when she resigned left him in an even worse position than if hadn't given her all those most important and difficult assignments, that he should have spread around the office. Now the other workers had to start from the beginning before they even reached the point where Peggy left off, causing delays that reflected on him even more and aggravated his precarious position with upper management. She hadn't been the only female employee to have complained, but had been one of the most vocal workers at the company, and had filed several complaints with government agencies placing the company under scrutiny and especially him. He bid his time as his anger slowly grew, especially after he was demoted to a lower paying position than what he had been promoted to, and now was only in charge of himself as he was given a corner office virtually away from everyone. He plotted his revenge and just what he would do, someday as his personal world began to crumble around him.

Roger checked on the progress of the painter as he completed the upstairs bedrooms, he was very satisfied when it was all completed. He also had Susan and Peggy inspect the bedrooms and living room before any furniture was moved in. They both were very satisfied with the highly professional job. Roger sent the painter a thank you note with a small token of his appreciation, a two hundred dollar check. A couple days later the furniture store was notified and soon delivered and set up the large bedroom sets along with the seating for both bedrooms and the rugs, twin couch sets and other furniture for the living room. Peggy and Susan were elated with the new bedroom locations and soon put the housekeeping staff to work moving their closets contents to the upstairs bedrooms. It took more than a week for the complete move, especially for Rogers and even more time for Susan's closet contents to be moved upstairs. When it was all completed, Peggy hugged Roger and said this was their bedroom together. They all loved it and had more space and a much better view of the city scape, and beside they could just walk out into the large living room and Roger had better access to the wet bar now and they could walk out onto the terrace at any time.

Roger and Peggy talked about where they should go on their honeymoon and after eliminating several destinations, decided on Miami Beach for a short seven day adventure. It was Peggy who didn't want to be gone from work to long and told Roger how much she enjoyed their life and working together, and planning the business, saying she loved him and their lives together. Roger wasn't all that excited with leaving either and being away from his new creation and real baby, the ROWE Company. Peggy enjoyed being a big part and neither one wanted to really leave and be away from Susan for any extended time. Besides they had all anyone would want, money, respect and one another's undying love and affection.

As the big day rapidly approached, probably the two least excited people were Roger and Peggy, they were happier as the most important day of their lives grew closer as everyone prepared for the big event. The week before their marriage was especially special for Peggy, as Roger took her shopping for their trip to Miami and she purchased a couple of casual summer outfits to wear. They spent the day together and returned home happy as they laid in their new bed and talked about the future, and discussed having children. Peggy said that maybe Anne was right about having them while she was young and getting it out of the way and asked Roger if he was ready to become a father. He said to Peggy it would and should be fun since they had plenty of help, and it shouldn't be too very difficult. Peggy asked, are you really ready? Roger responded no, and said he would never really be ready, and said all the people he knew who had children, and even the ones who had planned, never were really ready for the experience. But said they needed to have children, at least two and said he was ready if she was, since she would be the one who had to do all the work carrying them. Said he could imagine it would be a trying experience and he would love her no matter what happened. He made love to her but refrained from coming inside of her as they said they would wait until after the marriage ceremony before formally working on a family. Peggy said she wanted to have a short period where she would abstain from drinking alcohol so as to not complicate her pregnancy because she wanted to have healthy, happy children and would soon start after they returned from their honeymoon. After a short shower together they went downstairs and had dinner with Susan after she came home and told her some of what they had decided. After they finished eating, they all returned upstairs after Susan had changed her clothes, they sat and talked more. Susan said she had mapped out a strategy for opening several more restaurants under the Passion Fruit name and maybe a couple of the others of their existing brand names, and all that was needed now were some prime locations but would wait until Peggy could assist her and that would be after their wedding and honeymoon. Roger proposed a toast to a long a prosperous life together as they raised their glasses and cheered.

The Saturday before the wedding seemed kind of hectic for Peggy as she told Susan she was now starting to get nervous, even though they had planned and knew what was going to happen. Peggy's mother came over and she was more excited than Peggy, they had lunch together and Mrs. Thomas talked, it seemed like the entire time she was there. They took her to the upstairs living room and then to the terrace and fixed her a couple of drinks and she seemed to calm down a little. That evening after Sarah Thomas had left, Peggy was truly relieved and fixed herself a nice stiff drink, and said she needed some rest after such a mentally challenging and stressful day as she and Susan went to Susan's bedroom. Susan gave her a rubdown to help her relax after they both undressed. Susan applied massage oils to Peggy and soon she was sound asleep. Susan dressed and left Peggy sleeping and sat with Roger after he soon came upstairs and they sat and talked. Roger said he would be so relieved when it was all over and they could resume their normal routine as he told Susan that Peggy had decided she didn't want to be away from her or work too long. Roger said he had arraigned for them to take a private charter flight to Miami also. And just to avoid the hassle of the airport lines and check in, and besides they could well afford it. Susan said she wished she could go with them but that wouldn't be right but maybe latter they could plan a short trip together to somewhere special. Roger said he would welcome that and was sure Peggy would also as they have grown closer now and were all very happy together.

A couple hours later Peggy woke, and wearing just a robe came out and sat next to Roger as he held her and felt her warm body as she became excited. She stood and took him to the bedroom where they made love then showered and soon went to sleep.

The big day finally came as they went downstairs to breakfast and the three of them ate together as usual. Susan could hear the tiny bells in the distance as she finished eating and went and found Min cleaning the downstairs bedrooms. She checked her piercings and found them still in place and asked Min if she had followed Rogers's instructions as far as keeping them clean. Min said yes mistress and Susan told her that today she was to wear her smock because of the guess that would be here and to go put it on now. Susan checked the house and made sure all the beds were made up and clean before she went upstairs to her room to prepare herself for the wedding. Susan went and prepared to shower when to her surprise Peggy came and joined her as they bathed each other and Peggy asked her to take her as they engaged in some steamy bathroom sex as Peggy said it would help relieve some of the anxiety that had built up. They soon climaxed together several times while kissing then dried each other off going to the bedroom as they oiled one another. Peggy put her robe back on and kissed Susan and was glad she was in her life and thanked her for being here for her. They hugged, cried and kissed as Susan said it will be over very soon sister. They kissed each other passionately on the lips before Peggy headed to her bedroom to dress. Peggy began to dress and soon Susan came in her bedroom and helped her with all she needed done. It was getting close to the time they were to leave. Roger had dressed and kissed her and went downstairs and called for the limousine. Soon she was ready and they all prepared to go downstairs and the three of them entered the elevator and when they arrived downstairs, and the elevator doors opened some of the employees had gathered and they were clapping and cheering as they exited through the front entrance of the building. Roger and Anne White had departed several minutes before them as they went and stepped into the waiting limousine and headed to the nearby church. When they arrived they were greeted by some of the invited guest standing outside as they entered the church and had about twenty minutes before the ceremony was to begin. Peggy's father kissed her as she entered the church, then her mother as they went to a side room and prepared for the ceremony. Mrs. Thomas went and took her seat inside as did Rogers parents and Roger went and stood in the front of the church. Then Peggy was walked down the aisle with her very happy and smiling father. Soon she stood across from Roger and the reverend Timothy Jones officiated the simple and short ceremony as they soon placed the rings on one another's fingers, as the reverend pronounced them man and wife, they kissed and walked down the aisle together. Now Peggy was Mrs. Peggy Sue White and was all smiles as they exited the church to an ecstatic applause and camera flashes. They entered the limousine as Susan rode with their parents and they headed for the Town and Country restaurant. Susan was on the phone and had the staff on standby as they quickly arrived. The restaurant was decorated but not overly done as per Peggy's instructions, though Susan had it nicely decorated and had a seven piece band playing when they arrived. There was a banquet table for the bride and groom with both their parents on either side as Champaign was served.

The reception lasted about five hours and when it was over everyone was happy and fully satisfied since a complete meal was served with various selections to choose from and for sure no one went home hungry. Susan was last to leave as she made sure the restaurant was made ready for its regular night of business and had brought in extra staff to help for the special occasion. Before she departed, made sure she had a detailed list and noted all the employees who had made it such a success and they would be receiving a bonus with their regular checks. Susan headed home tired but knew it was worth it for her brother and that she would do anything for him and also Peggy.

When Susan finally arrived home she went straight to her bedroom, undressed and took a hot shower and went straight to bed. When she awoke the following morning she found herself between Roger and Peggy, and started to cry as they both held and kissed her, and when she finished crying they thanked her for all she had done and helped her out of bed and said they would be waiting for her downstairs to have breakfast. They ate together and Peggy said she was packed and they would be leaving around noon. When Roger finished eating he called and arraigned for the limousine to pick them up an hour before their flight. They finished eating and then went to get themselves together for their flight and Susan said she would miss them both as everyone dressed. Susan asked if she could go to the airport with them and they said they would welcome it very much. They gathered their bags and headed downstairs to the waiting limousine. The trip didn't take long since they were leaving from the in town airport that handled small private planes. They checked in at the small terminal and were soon led to a waiting private jet for hire. Roger and Peggy kissed a tearful Susan and went and boarded the small jet aircraft, as Susan waited until they were airborne before returning to the auto and heading home. For Susan it was one of the only times in several years since college that she wasn't near her very dear brother and more than a year since Peggy had come into their lives and now would be all alone and thought about how much she loved them both and were her closest family and prayed nothing ever happened to either one of them. Susan spent the day reading and going over company records to keep herself busy.

Even though they both had flown in the past, neither had ever flown on a privately chartered flight, this was a first for both of them as they held hands. The flight would only take about two and a half hours and they would land at another private air field and go directly to the beach front hotel with a fantastic view that Roger had booked and directly to the bridal suit for their weeklong stay. The flight went well as they landed and the happy couple exited the aircraft. Roger immediately called Susan to let her know they had arrived safely and told her they missed her already. Susan said she loved them and to enjoy themselves. Roger and Peggy headed to the waiting limousine and headed to their hotel. Once they arrived and checked in they were surprised their room was at the very top, one floor below the top floor which was the sun deck with a bar and small bistro. They unpacked and held each other and kissed and Roger asked Mrs. White, what did she want to do, and Peggy said she just wanted to walk along the beach and then maybe have something to eat. The weather was warm as the ocean breeze made the extremely warm and humid temperatures very pleasant. They walked along the beach and then Peggy said let's look at some of the clubs that peppered the main street parallel to the ocean. Roger said to her, I know what you are doing, and she said what. He said getting more ideas for our restaurant business. She said you know me so very well Mr. White and that's very good because I know what's on your mind. He said what, she said you want me to get one of those string bikinis, and said its written all over your face as they soon came upon a store that sold them, and he had this big grin on his face. Peggy turned to him and said for you my love anything, as they went inside and soon she purchased several and said she had also purchased one for Susan. After leaving the beach front store they found a nice restaurant on the beach on their way back to the hotel and had a late lunch.

They enjoyed the food and returned to their hotel room and Peggy put on the new bikini and Roger was now very excited. It was very revealing and just covered the nipples of her small round breast and the small camel toe between her legs and said all she needed was to wear a light smock type jacket and would be considered fully dressed by the native inhabitant's standard of dress. Peggy took the bikini off and asked Roger to make love to her as they climbed into bed, and said she wanted him to come inside of her now since they were married and enjoyed feeling him inside of her as they made passionate love. Roger first began by performing oral sex on her as he slowly licked his way up her inner thigh as he reached her vagina and pressing his tong between the now moist lips and feeling around her clitoris as it soon came out of hiding, licking and squeezing it between his lips, and soon bringing her to a rousing climax before he continued kissing his way up her body and slowly climbed his way on top of her, then he slowly slid his manhood inside the very anxious and highly aroused Peggy, licking her ear as she squirmed and slid deep into her woman hood and climaxed inside of her vagina filling her with his hot sperm for the very first time ever. The entire time they were on their honeymoon Roger came inside of her, as Peggy informed him they were making their family now as they truly enjoyed sex with one another. They had a wonderful time walking the beach and enjoying the night life as Peggy and Roger talked and they were intrigued by the numerous and various clubs that dotted the wide tree lined streets. The seven days seemed to pass very quick for the happy couple, but they both expressed a burning desire to return home, and both missed Susan's close and constant companionship very much. Soon they boarded the private plane for their return trip and into the waiting arms of Susan after they landed back home. Susan was waiting for them at the small airport and was so very happy to see them return, she was in tears. They rode back home and when Peggy handed Susan the bikini she went and put it on immediately and returned, as Peggy put hers on and they went and laid out on the terrace in the evening sun. Peggy said she let Roger come inside of her and hoped she soon became pregnant. Susan said she was so happy for her and them both as they celebrated and Peggy told her about some of the restaurants and clubs she had visited and had some new and very different concepts for some of their restaurants.

Peggy and Roger both were happy to return to work and Susan had the latest issue of the local real estate magazine. It had an in-depth article updating the latest changes at the ROWE Company, and it also mentioned the marriage of Ms. Thomas to Mr. White and her promotion to CFO and Roger now as chairman of the board and Ms. Stone as CEO and said since the last time the magazine had reported on the ROWE Company they were looking to expand a new chain of restaurants and might possibly soon be offering franchises to qualified investors. Peggy asked where did they get their information from, and Susan said directly from her. Said she had an interview with one of their reporters and said it was good for women to know they had the opportunity to break the glass ceiling and it should be an inspiration for even more women in business to not give up and press ahead with their dreams, hopes and aspirations. There was the exclusive interview Susan had given and it quoted her verbatim and was a very positive interview for all the women in the business community.

Several weeks had now passed before Peggy went to the doctor after she missed her period and had a pregnancy test performed, the doctor informed her she was pregnant, she was elated and headed home with the happy news and couldn't wait to tell Roger, Susan and the rest of the family. When she arrived home she was the first, she went and changed clothes and waited for Roger to arrive from work, and knew he would be home soon along with Susan. She would inform Roger and Susan and then go next door an give Anne and Roger Sr. the happy news. It wasn't long before Roger and Susan arrived and she told them the good news, he hugged and kissed her with a broad smile on his face before they went next door to inform Anne and his dad. They were very elated to hear the happy news and celebrated as Peggy said she wasn't drinking because she wanted to have the healthiest baby or babies possible. They returned home and settled into their usual routine as Peggy and Susan sat and talked about opening some new restaurants and where they might be located along with other interesting subjects.

Chapter Fifteen

The weeks quickly passed as Susan and Peggy formulated their plans for the expansion of the Passion Fruit brand, as the chain they decided would have the best overall appeal as a part of their well-planned major expansion. This was partially based on a walk-in customer survey, an in-depth review of overall revenue, popularity, and generational appeal, and the type of restaurant they felt would have the best chance of success over all their other restaurants brands to fit into a variety of different and diverse neighborhoods. They decided not to do any franchises until they could judge overall demand first, and see how well it grew, and what appeal it had in different and varied locations. Then maybe just spin it off one day or operate it as a separate entity altogether if they ever decided to go nationwide, or even start with another one of their now famous and popular brand name restaurants. They had formulated an expansion plan for several of the other brands also, but at a much slower pace just to see what would happen and had opened another Rock House in a trendy neighborhood and it was doing very well, and opened three more compared to the seven Passion Fruits opened over the same time period. Susan had decided to only keep the reserved booths at the original restaurants more because they were the closest ones to home and they both had decided to one day do away with them completely. They decided not to have any at of the newly opened locations that were now scattered all around the vast city, suburbs and were now spreading statewide. Susan and Peggy did continue to make spot checks on a semi regular basis of all the various locations they could, but on a less frequent basis that had turned out to be even more random now than before than when they first started out, as the number of locations continued to grow now to other far flung locations in the tri state area and beyond. The company debt continued to go down and the debt almost all but disappeared, until they decided to invest in the development of the old warehouse site that Roger had demolished and had started construction on. The new development he planned actually doubled in size before construction started, and the cost of the investment was very significant, close to a billion dollars and was the largest and most expensive new project to date in the city. When completed it would be the premier place to be, it was a big gamble, but Roger was willing to take it and he would succeed. Many articles had been written about it and the huge gamble Roger was taking on in the process of its development. Peggy went every week and checked on the warehouse operations, most of the time she went alone and took a ride share vehicle because of the convenience and cost and on some occasions Susan would go with her.

As the weeks turned to months and by the time Peggy was half way through her pregnancy they had opened five more new Passion Fruit locations and three new Rock House locations, and only two were within walking distance of one another. Peggy worked a half day now and saw her doctor on a regular basis and Susan was right there with her just about every time she went. They had become inseparable now and at home as they pleased each other sexually on a regular basis. The three of them were very close and very happy together.

One weekend they all went and spent time with Susan's mother, Ethel Anne and Roger Sr. as they spent some time at their summer home about ninety miles away in the wooded hamlet of Pikesville. They had a marvelous time as they lounged around, walked and sailed on the fairly large lake that bordered the property. Anne White loved treating Peggy to the different dishes she had prepared herself as they enjoyed one another's company. Peggy was just starting too really show as Susan and her shopped for maternity clothes. Her face was starting to show the signs of pregnancy as well as her breast and Roger loved lying in bed with her as she grew larger, rubbing on her stomach as they both talked to the unborn baby. She did complain about not being able to lay certain ways but other than that she was having a very normal and uncomplicated pregnancy. They went to the country house several times during Peggy's pregnancy so she could relax and unwind from the everyday pace she had set for herself.

By the eighth month Peggy was working from home as she continued to monitor company operations remotely as she and Susan were very happy with their expansion plans as their profits increased and the popularity of each new location increased also. Ethel Anne would check on Peggy almost every day since having grandchildren was something her and Roger Sr. had very much hoped for and very much looked forward to and especially having little ones running around and were probably more anxious than both Roger or Peggy. It wasn't long before Peggy was headed to the hospital and after her water broke she soon delivered a healthy baby girl, she weighed close to six pounds. Peggy was relieved and held her baby girl and soon began breast feeding her. Peggy believed in having a healthy child and had abstained from drinking and taking any types of medications. They named the baby Sarah Anne after Peggy's mother and her other grandmother Anne. She was a beautiful baby girl and Roger was overjoyed at having an heir to his growing fortune as was the entire family. Peggy insisted they not spoil her and was very old fashion in her beliefs of child rearing. Peggy breastfed the child and she grew to be very strong and showed early signs of being exceptionally intelligence. After the initial first few weeks Peggy was working to rid herself of the weight and physical signs of child bearing and exercised on a daily basis. Roger was pleased as her breast had gotten slightly larger and they couldn't wait to return to their normal sexual activities.

Peggy soon returned to work since she had a nanny and Susan also was always around to help. They watched Sarah Ann grow, as Peggy went to the doctor on a regular basis to be sure the child was healthy and wasn't impaired in any way. Four months after Sarah Anne was born Peggy found out she was pregnant again; Roger was elated and hoped they would have a son this time. Well his wish soon came through nine months later when Robert Walter was born, named after her father and Rogers. Peggy reassured him that was it as far as having children went and began her extensive exercise program all over again, working out again daily and within six months you would have never guessed Peggy had ever been pregnant as she was again her cute and slim self. Walter Roger was breast feed also and grew to become a very healthy child. Six months after his birth Peggy had all but returned to her pre pregnancy weight and dress size. She was very happy with her appearance now as her figure had now filled out; she had that beautiful very feminine mature look about herself. Roger said she looked better now than before which made her feel really good. She stressed the point that she was through having children and said two was enough and they would have to return to having sex like before they were married. He agreed with her and had no problem with it, and having the two children so close together proved to be a real advantage for them both since they were right behind one another as to walking, talking and toilet training and very soon school, and it wasn't long before they started going to preschool.

As Roger, Peggy and Susan continued to build and expand their company and soon the buildings on the site of the old factory and warehouse were finally completed, and Roger named it, the Rivers Bend City Center. He named it that because of its location right at the major bend in the river that a portion of the property bordered. After taking almost five years from the start of demolition, to completion of the very last building, it was now one of the most marveled at real estate developments to be completed in the past decade and of course in recent years, with its mixed use of different well planned and designed buildings and its open space with a park like setting. It was so well designed it was deemed an architectural master piece with its state of the art facilities as it was written about and praised worldwide as the future direction of the change now happening in many older city landscapes around the world. A Passion Fruit and a Rock House restaurant both were opened at Rivers Bend with new restaurants located on opposite ends of the development, and within walking distance of one another with the last minute addition of a Barrier Reef in between the other two locations. It occupied such a large track of land that they were more than two city blocks apart and proved very popular and beneficial for the neighborhood and the other surrounding business since it provided a variety of dining experiences as it attracted a variety of different patrons. People who dined there experienced a variety of different but very entertaining eating atmospheres. It proved so successful that, Peggy and Susan decided after they were open after several months and looked at the revenue wondered if this twin combination could be applied to some of the other various locations. They tried it at only two other similar locations because of similarities and it seemed to be the right combination as one complimented the other.

One weekend Peggy and Susan while sleeping in Peggy's bed decided they wanted Min to service them, as Susan said to Peggy she was glad her freaky side had come back to her, it had been more than a year due to her two pregnancies. Peggy said now that the child birthing phase was out of the way she wanted to be herself again. They called for Min, Susan had been having her while Peggy was pregnant, and Peggy had abstained as she didn't want to chance complicating her pregnancy in any way. Min soon appeared as they closed the door and ordered her to undress. Susan inspected her closely and especially her piercing, they had taken well and Roger had over time increased the size of the rings that adorned her small beautiful and petite body. Peggy and Susan undressed and Min knew what was in store for her, knew she would have to pleasure both women and they would take full advantage of her and was happy as they did so and saw that Susan had a strap on dildo nearby. Peggy lay on her back as Susan told Min to service her mistress as she climbed into the bed between Peggy's now spread legs and began to lick her vagina as Susan pushed her head down and stood behind Min with a leather strap in her hand as she began spanking Mins buttocks. Min preformed as she was expected and had done so many times in the past, this was no exception and Peggy soon climaxed. Susan then lay on the bed next to Peggy as they kissed and Min serviced her also, and she soon climaxed. Susan stood, reaching over and putting on the strap on harness with the attached dildo and with Min bent over applied some lubricant to her before entering her vagina. Min soon climaxed and then Susan stuck it in her anus while Peggy played with her clit as Min climaxed again. They turned her over on her back as they took turns sitting on her face as she licked their vagina an asses as they enjoyed abusing the subservient Min. Min over time had come to enjoy Susan's sexual abuse and also Peggy's but really liked it even more when Roger took her as he was more gentle in his treatment of her. They took her to the shower where she was made to kneel as they urinated in her mouth, before having her bath them both. They were satisfied after they all bathed, and had her apply massage oil to them afterwards. Then they oiled Min as they felt all over her, pulling her rings and having their way with her as she climaxed several more times before they had her dress and leave as they hugged and felt on one another before going to the living room and fixing themselves a drink as Peggy said she really missed having her sexual adventures with Susan, even though they had sleep together through her pregnancies it just wasn't the same.

Chapter Sixteen

As the months passed, and began turning into years soon it was Sarah Anne's second birthday as everyone celebrated the occasion and both sets of grandparents had been over joyed at having the two new additions to both their families. Peggy's parents came to celebrate little Sara Anne's big day, showering her with even more gifts. Roger Sr. and Bob Thomas retreated to the library after the cake was cut and had a couple drinks, as they joked around and discussed the markets. A couple hours later the festivities were over and a happy Bob and Sarah Thomas returned home. One thing for sure Peggy knew the children would be well loved and taken care of if anything ever happened to her. They returned next door to their apartment as Susan and Peggy discussed expanding there restaurant empire even more. Roger had looked at some prominent properties in other major cities and decided with the capitol reserves they had acquired in the past few years; it would be beneficial to invest elsewhere besides being so heavily invested in their local markets and decided to create a new trust to hold some of the newly acquired properties. While he discussed the acquisition of more properties they were also deciding on which restaurant brands to expand to other major cities nationwide.

As Susan and Peggy continued with building their empire of restaurants, Roger was moving in a new direction as his real estate investments were turning now more into new developments, as he began several new construction projects. None of them were aware of being the center of attention of anyone who might be planning to do them harm. But one individual did as his plot of revenge and retribution was slowly building as it was soon in the near future about to be put into action. The plan he was hatching was about to move forward and had been in the planning stages for several years now. At least now the movements of his main target of retribution had developed somewhat of a regular routine. It would take cunning and perfect timing to pull off his long awaited plan of revenge.

Roger now held one of the vice president positions at the White Company, and soon after asked his dad for a position on the board of directors, since ROWE was valued at well over a couple billion dollars with all its combined assets and holdings and had far exceeded the White Company in value and demanded more of his daily attention and time. The White company was more of an asset management company, where ROWE consisted of the actual hard assets. Roger Sr. approved his request and soon after Roger just sat on the board which actually gave him more time to manage his own company's direction and daily operations. Roger soon created two new REITs and by the time Robert Walter was two going on three years old. Roger had actually created four so all the company assets would be spread around, and all were individually valued at over five hundred million or more each and included properties located all over the country, Canada and some in South America as well as investments in Asia. Roger created trust funds for both his children through the White company and his dad took personal interest in managing both funds since Roger just turned over cash, and bonds into both children's funds.

He now made an annual contribution to the White Charitable trust, with Susan and Peggy's input since both had seats on the board. The restaurant empire continued to grow and so did the club card along with them and soon the third floor was fully occupied and operational and was completely devoted to just the card and restaurant operations. Peggy had virtually staffed the entire department with former colleagues from Harbor, and they were some of the most capable and reliable people you would ever find anywhere. Rogers's operations and acquisitions were continuing to expand even more as he diversified their holding. Peggy, Roger and Susan soon took a short vacation together after they had completed assembling one of the most capable management teams possible to manage the day to day and most important company operations in their absence. They continued to oversee every aspect of the operation, but the day to day decisions were left to the management team they had so carefully over time assembled. They went to the office daily, but their work hours were more varied than everyone else. They each maintained hands on management style, and was the real reason for their continued success. They held weekly meeting with the team in there large and most modern board room.

Peggy continued to oversee in person, once a week the warehouse operation and especially after it was expanded, doubling in size due to the opening of more than seventy new restaurants and with some locations being located further away. Peggy called as usual for her usual ride share pickup and was always going either on Tuesday or Wednesday to personally check on operations and plan improvements or check on any changes in its operations. She really liked being in touch with the managers as she checked the building and various operations and was always present when it was inspected by the health department, city or state and all the warehouse employees liked her and knew she took a personal interest in the operation and their wellbeing and meet with the union stewards just about every time she visited, they respected her and the way she operated. It was the best run operation of its kind in the entire country and had even won several top awards and was a leader in setting industry standards. Peggy was very proud of the operation; this was really her first baby, and had no reason or intention of changing her management style since several articles had been written about its operation and being a woman in a male dominated industry brought her respect and notoriety in the field of warehouse and food distribution management.

It was one balmy day, a light rain had fallen earlier as the temperature was pleasant, and it was a Tuesday, the day when Peggy usually went to oversee and inspect the warehouse operations and engage with its staff and called around her usual time for her ride share, using a well know and reliable ride share app. She was satisfied using the ride shares and never paid too much attention to the drivers after getting in, and after giving them her destination. Today she was going to inspect the new freezers that had been installed and the additional backup power units since the operation had now doubled in its physical size because of the addition of the rapidly expanding and varied restaurant operations. Susan was busy in the board room as she listened to a preliminary bank presentation on streamlining the card operation that was presented by a regional bank representative who's bank wanted a cut of their independent card operation that Suanne enterprises operated, otherwise she would have gone with Peggy, but she hadn't visited the warehouse in a couple months anyway and always felt Peggy had it well under control. It was on this fateful day that Peggy's nemesis would suddenly strike and catch her truly by surprise. Peggy's life was a very happy and secure one, and never would have imagined that anyone would want to do her any physical harm. As usual, Roger was just as busy as Susan, as Peggy headed downstairs on the elevator and out the front lobby just as her ride share pulled up, or so she thought. The driver got out and opened the back door for her, after the driver returned to the driver's seat; Peggy gave him the address to her destination as he pulled off. Peggy had no clue that the driver wasn't the one who had been dispatched to pick her up. Her driver watched her intently through the rear view mirror as the malice and disdain he felt for her began to really build up in his sick mind now that he had her in his demented clutches. He hadn't been this close to her since she worked at Harbor as he could smell the faint odor of her perfume as it pissed him off even more. Peggy wouldn't have recognized him anyway since he was wearing a skillfully made facial disguise. And besides the last few years had taken a physical told on him as his once pleasing appearance, began to change as his deep and intense inner hatred had grown inside of him and that caused him to have many sleepless nights as his life continued to deteriorate and spiral downward and out of control ever since the fateful day she resigned. He blamed her for all the disgusting changes in his life over the past four almost five years now, and her continued success as he followed her closely in the newspapers and business journals and magazines didn't help. Time had passed as his hatred had just grown and festered, just like a blister or boil, and it was ripe and ready to burst, and today was going to be the start of that day. One minutes after he had pulled off the actual assigned driver pulled up in front of ROWE headquarters, he had driven Peggy on several different occasions and got out of his auto and began looking around for her, after a couple minutes he texted back to dispatch that there was no pick up here, it was unlike her to not show after making arrangements for a pickup and texted back that she was a no show, and was quickly assigned to another location since it was very busy that particular day.

Peggy only occasionally glanced up as she looked at her cell phone checking on several different individual restaurant operations and some of their running warehouse accounts tracking there operations closely and paying little to no attention to the quickly passing urban landscape until the driver quickly pulled off and into a dark abandoned industrial building, stopping suddenly, and quickly jumping out and then entering the rear passenger compartment with her, catching her totally by surprise, as he quickly covered her face with a heavily soaked chloroform rag, she passed out very quickly as she took deep breaths by being so surprised. Her resistance to the quick attack was little to none and in vain as she was overpowered by the very strong and much motivated by hate former boss man. Her nemesis was no other than her ex-boss, Mr. Samuel J. Wine. He then covered her eyes with a blindfold and quickly cuffed her wrist behind her. He took her phone, which had fallen onto the cars floor and turned it off and removed the battery. He went through her purse, taking the cash from her wallet, and then pushed her down on the back seat, before covering her with a blanket he quickly retrieved from the trunk. He returned to the driver's seat as he now drove to the final destination where he would put in place the final stages of his sick, and diabolical plan of revenge and retribution on a most undeserving and innocent human being. Peggy had felt intimidated by his presence at Harbor as he seemed to have picked her out from all the other females and directed his very unwanted attentions toward her. He would stand over her and on several occasions when very few of her coworkers were around stand very close to her with his crotch very close to her face; it's these incidents which he had repeated several times over the course of her employment that led her to reporting him to upper management in the company.

He had watched her very closely and always began keeping up with her after her resignation from Harbor and found it almost unavoidable not to find an article in the business sections of the newspapers or local business journals about the ROWE Company, and especially after making its very public debut and her personal involvement in its expanding and successful operation, and now she was the CFO, that struck a sore nerve. He

would never forget that day when she resigned, when
Roger told him she would be the general manager, and be
paid several hundred thousand dollars, and the insult he
felt when Roger told him to crawl back into the hole he
called and office. Then the embarrassment he felt as his
employees sneered at him for weeks afterwards, then
within several short months his best employees were
skimmed off to work at ROWE, and for much better pay.
Then when he was called upstairs to explain why his
department's productivity was taking such a nose dive,
and his ultimate demotion. Then when she married Roger
White and read about his successes which really gnawed
at him and gave him ulcers. He began to drink more
heavily, his wife soon left him after the pay cut that went
with the demotion; they didn't get along very well
anyway even when things were going well for him. Then
she divorced him, calling him a looser and one sorry son
of a bitch. After losing his home in the divorce, and
having to sell and split the proceeds with his ex-wife, he
was at his wits end. He now felt he had been truly fucked
in the ass. The small amount of money he did get out of
the divorce after having to sell his gorgeous four
bedrooms home in an exclusive suburban neighborhood
did allow him to purchase his now current residence. It
wasn't in the best of shape when he bought it but wasn't
depilated to the point of not being repairable, it was a
frame house in a once vibrant neighborhood that now
was home to people like him, the down and almost out,
the working poor, and senior citizens who lived here
forever. He started making all the necessary repairs and
felt he had to start from scratch all over again, something

he hadn't planned on at this stage in his life, but shit happens, and that was what he had planned for Peggy White, the bitch CFO. He was doing better than most of his neighbors, he had a car, not the ones he used to cherish, the ex-got that as he ended up with a couple of used automobiles, one he had purchased was good enough for him to qualify to be a ride share driver, and wasn't doing too bad financially as he drove when he wanted. The other was a well-used minivan he purchased just so he could carry materials as he fixed up his new home and would use as he worked out his plan of revenge. He had been planning for a long time on just what he would do and after he purchased this house it all came together in his sick mind.

He finally reached his final destination, his now new home, as he backed up the slight hill and up the well-worn out over decade's driveway with its broken chunks of concrete and gravel, parking behind his house. In the back yard was an old forty foot shipping container next to the old unpainted garage that he used for extra storage of the various building materials he used to make his home habitable, drywall, particle board, plywood and buckets of drywall mud, 2x4s and some light fixtures he had replaced. When he stopped backing up, his auto was hidden and out of sight from the street, as he got out and went and closed the metal cyclone style fence gate he had just driven through. On his way back to the auto he unlocked the cellar doors behind the house and opened the large double metal doors, opening both after removing the large pad lock that held them secure. He then opened the back door to the auto and placed on the ground the blanket he had covered Peggy with, as he lifted the still unconscious Peggy from the auto, and laying her on top of the blanket, he then dragged it across the uneven ground with her on top until he reached the cellar door opening where he then picked her up from behind and carried her down the steep stairs into the very deep dark basement and laying her still unconscious body down on the dirty basement floor and turning on the lights as several florescent lamps came flickering to life and illuminating the entire basement. The house had been built in the late forties and the previous owners, several over the many past decades had added additions and one had even built a bomb shelter, it was here that he intended to keep Peggy White his prisoner as he would then put into play his next diabolical plan. He was going to possibly ransom her for money if he could, but really wasn't concerned with a ransom, his was more a plan of revenge, if they didn't pay, oh what the hell she would just have to die from neglect as he looked at her as she lay on the filthy basement floor, he really didn't care, all he wanted was his own personal satisfaction of revenge. He didn't care about anyone but her, she started it as far as he was concerned and wanted to embarrass and humiliate her anyway he could. He walked over to a hidden section of wall and it opened. It was a well-hidden secret section of wall, designed by who ever built it to be hidden, it would be difficult to find, without any prior knowledge of its existence. After opening it a large metal door was revealed and located down a short hallway about ten feet away, he unbolted it by grabbing a handle and sliding back the heavy metal bar that held it securely in place and opened it. There was another door, one which he had added, similar to a jail cell door, with bars made of construction rebar; it had a latch for a lock if he ever decided to have one. He opened both, revealing a room made of poured concrete and concrete blocks, it measured roughly twelve feet wide by eighteen feet deep with a height of nine feet, and inside was a rusty metal bed frame, probably army surplus, with sagging metal springs and a very thin and soiled mattress, a plastic bucket sat under what was once a chair, that was just legs now with a worn out toilet seat attached, that sat over the bucket. There was also a very small sink, similar to what dentist used to have with one faucet, and inside of it a small plastic cup from a water dispenser. A long metal chain was attached to the center of the ceiling between the two light bulbs with protective glass and metal covers. At the end of the long chain was attached a thick heavy metal collar that lay on the floor with several more feet of chain.

After opening the doors he returned to where Peggy was laying limp on the floor, she only had one shoe on as he thought about having to go back and remove her purse and all of her other personal items from the car, making sure he didn't leave any traces of her presence. He half dragged and half carried her into her new room, he lifted and placed her on the bed and removed the hand cuffs and blindfold, then slowly began removing all her clothes, he was truly enjoying this and received great satisfaction as he began cutting away the beautiful and very expensive clothing off of her with a fairly dull pocket knife as he threw the shredded and torn clothing in a pile on the floor with the satisfaction of a cat playing with a mouse until she was completely naked, he caressed her smooth and very beautiful body becoming highly excited. He pulled out of his pants, his short stubby almost deformed but now very erect penis and jerked himself off as he leered at Peggy laying there helpless before him as he quickly climaxed and some semen dripped on her torn clothing as he wiped some of his semen on her breast, his breathing became labored and difficult because of his disguise, he then wiped himself off with a handkerchief from his trousers pocket. He soon got hold of his carnal thoughts and then began removing all of her fine jewelry. When she was stripped of all her clothing and jewelry, even her wedding ring, he took the heavy metal collar that was lying on the floor and placed it around her slim neck and attached the heavy pad lock to it, he stood back and just looked at her, by masturbating he had relieved himself of some of the anxiety that had built up surrounding his now criminally insane actions. The room was cool, but not cold as he picked up all of her torn clothing and jewelry and departed down the hallway and depositing them on the nearby work bench in the attached basement, before returning with the dirty blanket as he threw it inside on the floor before closing the first door with the bars, and then the second and securing it with the sliding bar, before he then closed the hidden wall section sliding it back into place. The place where he kept her was sound proof and totally isolated and away from the main house, and was located in the back yard, six feet below ground, and ten feet away because the house was located on the side of a slight hill that the entire neighborhood was located on. Soon after he found this house and had purchased it, his neighbor who lived next door told him about the bomb shelter along with stories about the nineteen fifties and sixties when people were more concerned about a Russian nuclear attack than anything else. The old man had lived in his house next door close to seventy years, it had been his parents' home before that and grew up in the neighborhood and knew all that had happen in the surrounding area over the several past decades. He had since passed away and he doubted anyone else would be around to know about the hidden bomb shelter. Once Sam had found the hidden door and figured out how to open the door to the shelter, he found it fairly clean and dry, just mostly dusty and a little musty since it had been closed a very long time. He soon cleaned it up along with the rest of his new home making all the needed repairs. He traced out some of the electrical connections from the fuse box and found out the shelter had a ventilator and removed the blower that fed fresh air in, cleaned it up and found where it exhausted in the rear of the property as he made repairs to the system, good he thought how convenient if it began to smell from his plan of having a long term human occupation. It had only been a couple hours since he picked up Peggy White, as he went outside and finding her other shoe, retrieved her purse and all her other personal items and returned dumping the contents out on the work bench as he took all the cash that he now found in a side pocket of the purse and then reassembled all her belonging on the table and didn't think they missed her yet but would have to dispose of her belongings quickly, he had been wearing surgical gloves the entire time so he wouldn't leave any finger prints or DNA. He placed her badly torn clothes, shoes, purse and all her jewelry along with her cell phone in a large unmarked brown paper bag with handles from a grocery store. He went outside and closed the cellar doors and replaced the pad lock. He wouldn't have to use this entrance again as he went inside the back door carrying the paper bag. It was early evening, close to four o'clock as he entered the kitchen and began fixing his dinner as he turned on the television and watched a talk show until the news came on. Yes, Samuel J Wine was now going to have his revenge as he went outside briefly and double checked that he had cleaned his car and disposed of all the evidence of the presence of Peggy White; it wasn't his day to drive and made sure he didn't drive on Tuesdays since finding out her routine and especially after he found out she used the ride sharing services, and found out how to hi jack and intercept the ride shares signal especially once he had her cell phone number and had observed her many times as the same driver usually picked her up and around the same time. He was waiting that Tuesday right out front as he picked up the signal and was waiting for her. He congratulated himself at having accomplished and being able to catch her so off guard and was surprised with all the money the company had they didn't provide transportation for her or any of their other employees, but then again knowing business was about making money probably felt it wasn't worth the added expense.

Chapter Seventeen

It was late afternoon and getting close to the time when Peggy should have returned from the warehouse when Susan after the presentation for the club cards, informed the representative she would have to consult with the CFO before any decision would be made as he attempted to coerce her into a commitment. Susan was too sharp for his tactics and told him she would let him know before the week was out. Susan called Peggy's cell phone and it automatically went to voice mail, she didn't think anything of it and knew Peggy would very soon return her call. It wasn't very long after that Roger called Susan and asked if she had heard from Peggy. No she replied and informed him she had called her but the call went to voice mail. Roger then called and got the same result. He asked Susan what was on her itinerary for the day; Susan replied she usually went to the warehouse on Tuesdays or Wednesdays, but was pretty sure she went their today. After about an hour Susan then decided to call the warehouse and spoke directly to the warehouse manager. He stated the last time he had heard from Mrs. White was when Peggy called him well before lunch around ten am and said she would be stopping by very soon and was on her way there now to do her usual visual inspection of the new coolers, but she hadn't arrived yet and was still waiting for her arrival because he knew she wanted to see the new walk-in coolers and additional backup generators that had been installed and that were now operational since the warehouse expansion. He said maybe she stopped for lunch but felt it wasn't like her to come so late if she was still on her way. Susan agreed with him, thanked him and now began to become very concerned and knew this wasn't like Peggy to just be unavailable this long or just disappear. She went to Rogers's office very upset now and informed him that she never arrived for her warehouse inspection, and doubted she was having any problems with her cell phone. Susan said we need to call the police now, and said she had a very bad feeling about this, as she explained what the warehouse manager had told her. They called home and checked that everyone else was accounted for, the children, their parents and all of the help. Peggy was a happy person and had no reason to just up and run away and would never leave them and especially her beloved children. Roger said ok then and he called the police and informed them of the disappearance and possible kidnapping of his beautiful and loving wife. The police informed them they would need to come into the police station and make out a missing person's report. Roger called his father and informed him of the pending situation and Roger senior soon joined him and Susan as they all went together to the police station and made out a missing person's report.

It happens that a reporter for the local television station WXYZ was there doing a news story about a dangerous criminal who had just been apprehended and captured in a shootout, and was on the FBIs ten most wanted list and was now in police custody. She had just wrapped up her story when she recognized Susan, Roger and Roger Sr. from covering several philanthropic events and recognizing them from the newspapers and other publications and over heard there report on the missing

Mrs. Peggy White to the desk sergeant. Then when Roger said it could be a possible kidnaping, she began preparing to do an on the spot interview. The police usually just took the information and waited twenty four hours. But with Olivia Brown there she immediately called back to the news desk at her television station and informed them about what she had just overheard. They told her to stay put and do a report, get some video and get an interview if possible. It was because of the standing in the community that the story of Mrs. Peggy White missing, and a possible kidnapping that became the hottest news story of the day. The desk sergeant saw the television news station crew approach the Whites and begin to question them as he panicked and quickly called upstairs after Olivia Brown of WXYZ approached the Whites as they stood at the front desk and began her interview, and then he knew these weren't your everyday citizens as her camera man began taking pictures and very soon detectives hurriedly came from upstairs and several other men soon appeared, with one wearing an FBI jacket as they quickly escorted the Whites to an interview room out of sight. The FBI had a satellite office here because of the nearby financial district. Olivia Brown called back to her news desk and asked for instructions, they told her to stay put and get whatever and all the information she possibly could.

Samuel J Wine, had changed his name after finishing college from Weinstein, and soon had applied and was hired, and began doing clerical work, it was all he could get at the time, the economy was tight, jobs scares and he stuck it out until he could do better. One day by chance he ran into a former college associate who told him about some openings for college graduates at the then small startup records keeping company called Harbor and Associates, that's what also really pissed him off also, he had put in close to twenty five years with them, helping them grow from a six person operation to almost two hundred with three offices before they gave him a severance package and the boot, and all because of that now rich bitch in his dirty basement bomb shelter. He turned the television on and watched one of the evening talk shows that were always on before the early evening news came on. That is what he was really waiting for. They started with the usual everyday crime stories and about the dangerous and most wanted criminal who had been apprehended after a shootout where several officers were shot as he warmed his microwave dinner and soon sat down to eat. As he watched the news there was a late breaking story, the possible disappearance of heiress Mrs. Peggy White the CFO of the ROWE company. Reporter Olivia Brown said officials weren't ready to call it a kidnapping as of now since no ransom demand had been made as far as they could tell and she had only been missing a few hours. According to all the early reports it seems she just vanished. The report was very short with shots of Roger White Sr., and Roger White and Susan Stone White when they were at the police stations front desk as Olivia Brown stated they would stay on top of this possible breaking story. Sam looked and broke out in laughter as he watch and saw the stressed out faces of the family members on his small wall mounted flat screen television. He retrieved his laptop turning it on as he waited for it to boot up. He had Wi-Fi and had installed cameras all around the outside of his home, and inside. The two that were mounted inside the bomb shelter were separate from all the others and were password protected that now served as a prison cell as he watched the screen come to life. He checked his e-mails before he checked his cameras and brought up the shelter, Peggy was still unconscious as he zoomed in for a close-up and watched her beginning to slowly awaken, then sitting up and realizing she was completely naked, chained and realizing she had on no jewelry, as her rings and earrings had been removed. She screamed as she stood up and went toward the door, but was jerked back and could barely reach it as the chain attached to the ceiling and the heavy collar around her neck wouldn't allow her to go quite that far. Just far enough to touch the two side walls, the back wall and a little more than half way to the door as she looked around and saw the cameras. She screamed at them, and then began to cry, she walked around testing the boundary's that the chain would allow. There was water, but it was just above a trickle as it dripped, the toilet was the chair legs with the old worn out mounted toilet seat and a bucket that fit underneath. She looked around and saw the blanket on the floor, picked it up and wrapped herself in it before sitting on the bed with her knees in her chest, with her head down as she cried profusely. He watched her for a very long time before he began speaking through the cameras, and informed her she was a prisoner of circumstance, and her rich bitch stupid cunt ass would be here a very, very long time, and that she would die here, all because he hated her. She asked the voice what it wanted. It answered and the reply was, revenge bitch. The voice sounded very familiar, but she just couldn't place it, and started thinking and wondered who hated her enough to do this to her and go to these extremes. She hoped and prayed she would be found soon knowing Roger and Susan were looking for her as she began to accepted the dire circumstances she was in now. And even thought she was chained and isolated inside this cool bare room, the circumstance was starting to arouse her as she felt on herself and could also feel the cramps starting to come that signaled she was coming on her period and that stopped those thoughts from overtaking her thinking as she tried hard to remember who was behind the steel door and remember the voice and why they had brought her, for what purpose, and what were they going to do with or to her, what did they want.

Samuel Wine had made several very professional facial disguises, as he had prepared for this revenge and motivated kidnapping a long time and assumed there would be cameras everywhere and also become a person of interest. He would soon leave home and drop the paper bag filled with Peggy Whites clothing and jewelry where it would be readily found. He wanted to send shock waves through the family he so despised, but not as much as he despised and hated Peggy most of all, and who he personally blamed for everything negative that had ever happened in his life, feeling he was doing fairly well until she came into his world and upset the apple cart. He was up for a possible promotion which would have doubled his salary and placed him in a private office overseeing a complete branch instead of being the number three person at the location at the time of his rapid downfall, then this stupid cunt bitch reported him to management and also made reports to the EEOC, then she resigned as he had given her the most complex and difficult assignments, oh she really fucked him when she left abruptly without any warning. He thought he also could just forget about her being in the basement and that thought began to make him feel better all ready. He decided he would do her like the North Vietnamese did their American prisoners of war, a cup of water and a small bowl of rice once a day and he would drug the rice so she wouldn't be any trouble in case he wanted to do her some physical harm, possibly fuck her, or torture her, on top of the mental anguish he knew she was feeling and the despair the longer he held her. He really didn't care if she died as he now felt so much better that she was here and could do whatever he wanted to her, whenever he wanted. He finished eating his meager dinner before washing his face, and would wear his least deceptive disguise as he prepared to leave home. He locked up and secured the house before leaving home and driving near to where he had picked her up, and soon reached his destination after about an hour's drive, parking in a public parking garage just a few blocks away from ROWE headquarters. He put on his simple facial disguise and stepped out of his auto with the paper bag rolled up in his hand and walked down the two levels to the ground floor and the short two block walk to the plaza where the large letters ROWE were located in the wide plaza, a block before getting their he replaced the battery back into her cell phone and walked to the plaza, circling and approaching the letters from the intersection side, unseen by the building cameras that covered the wide plaza and soon after entering turned on her cell phone and quickly climbed up the low brick wall behind the park style benches and across the flower bed and setting the shopping bag inside the large letter O, turned around and climbed back down and briskly walked away in the same direction he came from and away from the building and circled the block in the opposite direction. He knew the first thing they would do, would be to try tracking her cell phone. He was very correct about that. And hour and a half later after he arrived back home, he showered and began drinking. He turned on the television to watch the ten o'clock news; it would be on within the hour. He was good and relaxed when the news came on. Olivia Brown was now standing at the ROWE headquarters plaza where she reported Mrs. Peggy White's cell phone had been recovered along with some of her personal items. She reported police wouldn't say what exactly what was found but were looking at surveillance photos to try and find out who placed the bag there inside the large letter O, she also reported no ransom demand had been made so far and police were hopeful she would be found very soon.

Chapter Eighteen

The Police and FBI worked together and quickly formed a small combined task force because this type of crime couldn't be allowed to happen to anyone and especially to a member of such a prominent and distinguished family as the Whites. The Whites had a reputation of unbiased generosity and had given to different charities through the White Charitable Trust and the police widows and orphans fund and the injured officers funds were two of the charities that were the beneficiaries of their generosity and had received numerous donations over a very long period of time over the many years dating back to the nineteen twenties. The small task force of less than a dozen dedicated officers mostly all experienced detectives were now looking at the surveillance tapes of the plaza and bulletins had been sent to all the city police precincts to be on the lookout for Peggy White. Police and FBI agents diligently looked over video from both from the ROWE and White buildings and all the street cameras and other nearby building security cameras trying to establish and get a handle on who, where, what and when the paper bag was left with every item Peggy White had worn that day. The following day now twenty four hours later two FBI agents and a pair of city detectives interviewed the entire small loyal group of current ROWE employees at the company headquarters, and even at the food distribution warehouse. Many were very upset and despondent about Peggy White missing and were scared something very terrible had happened to her because she was such a sweet and down to earth person. The following day,

Wednesday in the late afternoon after police had sent several pieces of her clothing to the lab for testing was when police brought both Susan and Roger to the police station and they were shown the contents of the bag that was found, or rather left on purpose. When they when into the room where the contents were spread out on a large table Susan screamed, a scream of pure anguish and one of untold grief, and had to be held up by two detectives to prevent her from collapsing to the floor as she shook and cried uncontrollably for a very long time. All the clothing had all been removed with a dull knife and it was very obvious to anyone who looked at the shredded pieces. Every piece of her fine jewelry that she had worn that day was there, her wedding and engagement rings which she never took off, her earrings, bracelet and her favorite necklace, even her shoes, and the torn and ripped pantyhose and panties sent chills through Susan as she now shook uncontrollably. Susan being a strong person and even a dominatrix was shaken to the core when she saw what was lying on the table before her on the white paper that had been placed down before the contents of the paper bag were shown to her and Roger. Roger just stood with his head in his hands and just cried profusely. Police said they hadn't found any blood, which gave them some hope that she was still alive, but said there was an unidentified stain that they had determined was semen and it was being tested and compared to their criminal DNA data base.

The White household's once happy atmosphere was now one of depression and sadness, as everyone was hopeful Peggy would soon be found as Roger Sr. went to work to try and keep his mind off of thinking about his beautiful daughter in law, and having the morbid thought of having to help raise his beloved grand children without their loving mother. Ethel Anne visited her grandchildren every day to try and prevent them from becoming melancholy by keeping their spirits up or either they came next door to visit grand mama at home, and just to reassure them everything would be alright to keep their minds off of their missing mother. They couldn't help but know something was terribly wrong as Susan was so despondent she just sat and cried, alone and even when she looked and hugged them. Everyone did their best to keep the children happy as much as possible as they asked for their mother every day. The FBI upon doing their investigation soon felt they might have a lead; it appeared to be a real long shot though since no ransom had been demanded, yet. Once they had her phone, they were able to track all her previous phone calls and especially the calls starting that day, and the two they found most important were to the warehouse and for the ride sharing service from the phones history. They of course tracked down the driver who had been dispatched and was assigned to pick her up that day, they interviewed him and searched his home an auto and downloaded his automobiles GPS and soon cleared him off the suspect list as he explained when he pulled up to the ROWE building she never appeared at the pickup point. He explained that she had ridden with him several times and knew her on site, and said she was one of the most pleasant people you would ever come in contact with. They back tracked all of her ride shares over the previous year and checked them against the billing records. They interviewed several other drivers who had driven Peggy on other occasions, searched their homes and autos. Several employees whom she had brought from Harbor and Associates mentioned to the police about when she resigned and how her ex-boss was so very upset and a couple of women who were the last of the people she had hired and had also worked at Harbor and Associates told of how her ex-boss was demoted and had eventually been let go, which presented to them another possible lead, when telling them how they had come to work at ROWE, and about the incident that brought them here, and suggested they should also talk to Roger and Susan about it since they were with her that fateful day. Both Roger and Susan were re-interviewed about that day when Peggy had resigned, and recalled the incident very vividly.

Samuel Wine watched Peggy on his laptop after the news went off as she walked around trying to keep from getting stiff as she did some exercises that the chain around her neck would allowed her to do, as he leered at and admired her nakedness, looking at her beautiful nude body and thought motherhood had made her even prettier than when she worked for him, she was thinner then and being nude he could really admire her true beauty as he masturbated again as he watched her exercise. There was the small plastic cup in the sink, one the size you would find at a water dispenser. He had no reason to keep or make her comfortable as he watched her place the small cup in the sink and turn the handle on as it ran just above a dribble as she watched the slow running water fill the small cup. She took and drank as much as she could, she needed to drink, and her throat was dry. Peggy had another very personal concern; it was time for her period. She had no sanitary napkins and no way to wash either; she was beginning to smell herself now and felt the cramps that usually signaled her period were soon coming down and she was a heavy bleeder and really detested being dirty and unable to wash herself, there was no toilet paper either and had used the bucket a couple times now as she had defecated and urinated earlier. There were no windows and the smell was almost overwhelming and the light bulbs in the ceiling stayed on constantly, she was starting to lose all sense of time as she lay down and covered herself with the dirty blanket and thought about her family and her small children, and cried herself to sleep. Sam went to bed and slept very well after powering down his lap top. He lay in his bed and knew the police would investigate him and would have to feed his prisoner soon and decided he would do it early in the morning and dump her pail and open the well-hidden air vent and run the blower to let some fresh air in the now prison cell shelter. Waking up very early Wednesday morning, Samuel started after brushing his teeth, breakfast for himself and prepared a single cup of rice that he would feed his new prisoner, exactly one cup of rice on a paper plate after taking out four powerful sleeping pills and opening the capsules and dumping the contents and mixing it into the rice before he placed it on the paper plate. It would be all the food she would receive along with a six ounce bottle of water. He went downstairs, opened the secret wall panel and turned on the power for the vent which exhausted the air from inside through a well-hidden vent fifty feet to the rear of the backyard. Sam had a cattle prod in his hand and assumed she would try attacking him if she could, as he opened the cell door, and observed Peggy lying on the bed as the stench soon went up his nostrils almost making him sick. She suddenly stood and ran toward him just as he suspected she would try doing as he just stood in the doorway as she quickly approached him with a very determined look in her eyes, as she approached him and standing just out of her reach pointed the cattle prod in his hands at her, giving her a full jolt as she just about reached him, the shock he administered struck her in the center of her chest and sent her reeling backwards as she was slammed hard against the back wall, and her stunned and naked body then slid down to the dirty floor, her crumpled form lay semi prostrated on the dirty floor as she looked up at him dazed, he could have killed her with the jolt he had administered, besides the force which she hit the wall was enough to knock anyone out. He then removed the waste bucket and returned after he had dumped and rinsed it out as Peggy remained crumpled on the dirty floor, with her back against the grimy wall. She started to speak, asking why was he was doing this to her? He told her, she had fucked his life up, and was going to pay the ultimate price for all of the humiliation he had suffered because of her. He turned and left, returning soon with a child's plastic play bucket of cold water and a really old worn-out wash cloth, telling her to clean herself nasty bitch ass up, because her ass was stinking and smelled like the piece of shit she was, he loved talking to her in a derogatory manner and this excited him knowing who she was. He turned and left, returning with her first of many only once daily rations yet to come of food and water, before saying have a nice day, bitchhhh. It was the way he said bitch that really and truly frightened her; she could hear the animosity and feel the hate in his voice when he spoke. He turned and closed the first door, then the second, then the secret hidden wall. He allowed the blower to run almost an hour more until he left for the day. He had powered up his lap top and turned the cell cameras on as he observed Peggy trying to crawl over to the plate of rice to begin eating, he felt good as he looked at her and thought maybe he should assault her while she is still breathing and figured if she survived a month it would be a real surprise. He turned his lap top off and placed it high on top of the kitchen cabinet out of sight knowing the cameras in the shelter had a memory card and he would see her every move, even if she passed away. The outdoor cameras were of a commercial consumer type with their own DVR.

He prepared to leave for work, turning off the basement blower that brought the fresh air inside the shelter now prison cell as he locked the door leading to the basement and departed as he headed for his auto and another day of being a happy ride share driver, a hustle that he was beginning to enjoy as it brought him in contact with different and many interesting people, and besides it was beginning to become fairly profitable for him. He also thought the police would have a difficult time finding him since the house was in his deceased mother's maiden name and his mailing address was a rundown apartment building two blocks away, in a twelve flat where he resided with some poor working people. He fit right in and didn't stand out and it was a one bedroom apartment and gave him the cover he needed for the diabolical plan he had formulated over the past several very difficult and depressing years, as he planned for and now executed his most diabolical plan of retribution at the person he so despised and hopefully planned so well so he wouldn't ever be caught. It was one of the reasons he didn't care about if Peggy White perished, he would be completely satisfied with his plan of retribution. He had furnished both the house and the one bed room apartment with used furniture some of it from motels and slept there occasionally, enough to be considered a regular resident above suspicion and the rent was really cheap and the landlord lived there also which was even more convenient since he paid his rent on time and in cash, which didn't present him with any problems.

The police and FBI were having a difficult time trying to track him down. They went to Harbor and associates and began tracking him down. No one currently there had any idea where he was or what happened to him since the last address was the home he shared with his ex-wife. They finally tracked her down and she said she had no idea where he was and didn't care anyway, and said he was a miserable person as they finally were able to track his legal residence down through the DMV and his mailing address through postal delivery records and soon were knocking at his apartment door. Later they found and tracked him down through the ride share service he drove for and asked him to come in for questioning. Samuel happily reported to the police station and acted as if he knew nothing as he was soon questioned, denying any knowledge of the Peggy White disappearance and didn't know who she was. And stated he remembered when he worked at Harbor a skinny girl named Peggy Thomas. He answered several other questions about where he was and this was verified after several of his neighbors were questioned later. Sam said he was sorry about Mrs. White's disappearance, leaving the police station looking glum until he got into his auto and busted out laughing with a big smile on his face, it had been three days and the authorities had no clue of her whereabouts. Samuel figured and planned on him being followed and continued his driving for the rest of the day before calling it quits, and stopping at a local supermarket for some food since he was going to stay at the apartment tonight. He was right about that as he noticed the same car following him half a day and then another until he reached the apartment. After arriving home, there was a knock at the door, he opened the door and his neighbor from next door told him about the police questioning almost everyone in the building about where he was Tuesday. He explained they thought he might have something to do with the disappearance of Peggy White. The neighbor said oh, and bid him a good night and departed.

Peggy after sitting a couple hours against the wall after being shocked with the cattle prod, mustered up her strength and began crawling over to the plate and began to eat some of the rice and drank water from the pale he brought for her to wash with, saving the small bottle of water. She ate several handfuls of the bitter tasting rice before she slowly collapsed and fell into a very deep sleep.

The police and FBI could wait a very long time, but this time it wasn't on there side. After spending a the night in the apartment, and having one of the best most restful sleeps in a very long time, Samuel left to go to work, spending half a day working and continued being on the lookout and assumed he was being followed just to be on the safe side, but decided to switch cars after parking in one of city's public parking garages. He slipped unseen from his vehicle after parking to another level in the same garage and soon arrived at the old minivan. He slipped inside and put on another of the facial disguises he had so carefully made using actors makeup and latex. He soon departed in the minivan undetected that was registered under an alias, driving right past the undercover detectives that were following him as they cruised around the garage looking for him or his car. When they found his car after almost half an hour, they realizing they had lost him and now reported in what had happened and that they found his auto parked. They didn't know where he had disappeared to and wondered if he went to a theater since there were several nearby but anyway an alert was put out to be on the lookout for Samuel J Wine, but not to detain him, he was just a person of interest now and a possible suspect in the disappearance of Peggy White.

Samuel returned to the house now where Peggy was being held parking his car inside the garage and closing the doors before unlocking and entering the back door. He went and brought his lap top down and turned it on as he went and viewed the outside surveillance system time recordings first, he noticed there hadn't been any unusual activity all day. Nothing appeared to be out of the ordinary; he could relax now and went and washed up before fixing a sandwich as the laptop now was fully booted up. Even though there was and alert out for him he was able to relax as he viewed the secret basement cell and observed Peggy laying on the floor, he could tell she was asleep and could hear her breathing through the cameras sound system and just looked at her. He thought this was just too easy, and thought about hurting her, but was afraid he would be caught with his guard down if he did. As he watched her, he noticed she hadn't eaten even half the rice and the pail of water was still nearly full, he knew she was sleeping from the drugs. He ate the sandwich before fixing himself some dinner and turned the television on. It was evening now and turned to the station with the most reliable news reports, and soon the news came on and there was the WXYZ news desk and they had and exclusive report, the White family were now offering a million dollar reward that led to the return of, or capture of persons involved in Peggy Whites disappearance. The reward was read by Roger White as Susan stood by his side unable to speak, they were much stressed out by this ordeal continued on, and it really showed, especially on Susan's Pretty face. The chief of police came on next and said those involved would be punished to the fullest extent of the law if and when they were found, as he answered questions from several reporters. They switched back to the studio and continued with the evening news broadcast. Sam thought about how well his plan of revenge was working and how they would never find her. He ate his sandwich, drank a cold beer and went and took a warm shower before he returned to watch some more television. This time he sat in the living room in his big lounge chair and soon fell asleep. When he woke it was almost midnight as he turned off the television, and went and got in his big bed, going back to sleep.

The following morning when Samuel J. Wine awoke, after washing his face and doing his regular morning bathroom routine, he fixed himself a hearty breakfast of bacon and eggs, toast with jelly and turned on the laptop again and waited for it to boot up, soon turning on the camera application and looking inside the bomb shelter turned prison, to his surprise Peggy was walking around the room as he watched her, she was a very pretty woman as he looked at her nude body, but he still despised her, she walked slowly before she sat on the bed and finished eating the last of the rice that was left from yesterday. She laid down as he watched as the paper plate fell from her now outstretched arm. The drugs had put her to sleep again; at least he figured she was since he had drugged the rice. He prepared another pot of rice, and when it was cooling, stirred in several more of the sleeping pill capsules after breaking them apart and empting the contents before placing the rice on another paper plate. By all accounts from looking at the camera feed, she was

sleeping soundly as he prepared to go downstairs to the
basement. He opened the basement door and went
downstairs, placing the plate on the dirty work bench and
turning on the ventilator as he went and opened the
hidden wall and then the steel doors as he entered her
cell, he had the cattle prod ready as he approached her
prostrated body, she didn't even bother with the blanket,
she was sound asleep. He took the waste bucket, she had
defecated and urinated in and there was also a large
amount of blood, he turned and looked at her and
grabbed her thin ankle and spread her legs open wide, he
saw the heavy amount of blood that had dripped down
her thighs and dried and figured she was on her
menstrual cycle as he placed her leg back down as he
stared at her vagina, thinking maybe if she wasn't
stinking so bad he would rape her, but then again he
could just jerk off looking at her since he had her where
he wanted. The room reeked of human waste as he went
and dumped and rinsed the bucket out again and was glad
he turned the blower on before he entered. After
replacing the bucket, he went and got a broom and swept
the rice and paper plate up taking and dumping it and
bringing in the fresh plate of drugged rice, an a new
small bottle of water and another fresh bucket of water
for her to wash with, if she ever woke up and stayed
awake long enough to wash herself, he really didn't care
if she did or didn't, he didn't have to smell her stinking
ass. He departed, closing all the doors and the wall
behind him. He would again leave the blower on until he
left again. He went upstairs and took his time dressing
and putting on his disguise again as he prepared to leave

soon. He started locking up and shut off the blower heading out the back door to the garage. He drove to another public parking garage four blocks away from where he left his other auto and removed his disguise making sure no one was around to observe him as he removed it and stashing it in a poly bag and placing it under the driver's seat, combed his thinning hair, put on his favorite baseball cap and departed. Walking to the elevator and taking it down to the ground floor and casually walked to the other public garage for his ride share for hire vehicle and would do some ride shares before noon. As he walked looking to check if he was followed, and soon entered the garage where his other auto was parked, walking up the stairs inside the parking garage as he looking casually around before walking to his auto. He observed no one as he got inside, started in up and backed out and after leaving the garage and turned on his ride share app and made himself available. He wasn't aware of the now very serious professional surveillance he was now under. When he disappeared and switched cars yesterday, it made him a person of interest if not the prime suspect as a hidden transmitter had been attached and placed under his auto. He did his usual morning driving routine taking several passengers to various locations and even one run to the airport before he called it a day and returning to the apartment where he received his mail; he had a cheap shredder as he disposed of the unwanted mail with his name on it. He decided to stay here until later as he fixed some ramen noodles, looked at some television and watched the evening news as they reported that they were still looking for the missing heiress, and had just found the nude body of a female floating in the river and was waiting for it to be identified. He finished eating and soon dosed off.

Back at police headquarters the chief of police conferred with Jack (hound dog) Abif from the FBI, and lieutenant Yasi (wildman) Brown, a street wise city detective as they reported on the slow progress in the case of Peggy White, and the prime suspect now under very close surveillance, and how he had supposedly had given them the slip yesterday but were beginning to have serious doubts as to his involvement. The chief instructed them to use all the available resources and to get this case solved as they were waiting to identify the nude female body found floating in the river, and another found in a stream several counties away. He dismissed them as they went and brought in an additional squad of six men to help watch Samuel J Wine; these were undercover police officers and they watched him even more closely even thought a tracking device had been attached to his auto while it was parked had yield nothing to go on.

Samuel awoke, checked his watch and the evening rush hour was now over as he refreshed himself and again headed out. He went and got in his car did a few more ride shares until close to midnight before he decided he would return to get his other auto when he noticed a squad car behind him and did some maneuvers to see if he was being followed, sure enough they were following him. He decided to go to the apartment instead as he headed home noticed a second car following him as he now stopped for gas. He went inside the convenience store and that's when he observed both vehicles that were behind him now parked next to one another before he exited the store. He knew then he was being followed for sure very closely and headed to the apartment. He didn't have to worry about his prisoner since she had water and food anyway. He arrived home to his apartment on the second floor and had an unobstructed view of the intersection outside his apartment building since his apartment was located at the very front corner and he could look up both streets for at least a block in either direction. He fixed himself dinner, took a warn shower and put on some comfortable clothes to lounge in. He left the living room lamp and television on as he went to his bedroom, closed the door as the room was in total darkness and took out a cheap pair of binoculars out of a drawer and eased over to the window and peered down both streets and it wasn't very long before he spotted the undercover police who were following him from earlier that evening, soon a second car pulled up as the first one pulled away and left. He now knew he was there prime suspect and also suspected they had bugged his car with a tracking device. He didn't worry as he returned to the living room and looked at the clock; it was eleven and decided to go to bed as he turned the lights and television off. As he laid there thinking he might try returning to the house tomorrow but that would depend on the police surveillance as he soon fell asleep. When he awoke the next morning, after washing up went and stood in the shadows and scanned both streets in both directions and soon spotted the police a block away as they sat in and unmarked auto, sipping coffee and eating donuts. Samuel decided it would be a long while before he returned to the house as he again took the binoculars and observed the police again as another car pulled up next to the parked auto, after a few minutes the parked auto pulled out and making a U-turn as the second auto pulled next to his parked auto and a man stepped out of the passenger side, walked to the rear and reached underneath and removed something Sam assumed was a tracking device as the man quickly got back in and they spread away.

Chapter Nineteen

Samuel Wine after observing the police that morning figured that they had given up on watching him but decided to play it safe since he assumed the police were just trying to lure him in since they had planted the device when his auto was parked and had given them the slip. He really didn't give a flying fuck about Peggy White and if she died from, starvation, neglect or whatever and figured the police were being obvious just to try and sucker him in. He decided he would play there game, as he left his apartment and got into his auto and pulled out and passed by the house and several blocks later observed another unmarked squad following him. It was just as he suspected they were trying to play him as he made himself available on the ride share platform. He did several pickups and even suspected some to be undercover cops based on their conversations about the missing Peggy White. He did half a day and went home to the apartment.

At police headquarters the search for Peggy White was leading nowhere as the decision was made that Samuel Wine wasn't involved as all the heavy surveillance directed at him was soon ended. It soon became obvious to Sam when this occurred but, continued for another twenty four hours before he felt secure enough and headed to the parking garage for his other auto after stopping and filling his gas tank. After parking again in the garage where the minivan was located, he sat in his car for half an hour before he stepped out waiting to see if he was followed, looking around, he quickly disappeared before heading to the parked minivan. He reached the minivan, slipped inside and donned his disguise and soon quickly left. Sam took no chances as he took and drove to the house in a very indirect route. When he finally reached the house it was late evening on Saturday, as her entered the house. Peggy had been in the cell now two days since he last checked on her. Samuel was glad to finally be here as he took down the laptop and turned it on; he would look at the video from the past couple days before he even went downstairs to check on his captive. The laptop soon booted up and he soon observed his captive as she sat on the toilet as she leaned against the wall for support as she was becoming weak from her ordeal and the horrific conditions, she sat crying as she was now losing weight and looking very despondent. She stood as she pulled on the chain hanging from the ceiling as she lifted her now weakened body and lowered herself before picking up the small amount of rice remaining in the paper plate from the floor and now sat on the filthy mattress eating the remaining small amount as she slowly stretched out as the paper plate soon fell from her hand, she was again asleep. Sam now decided to go downstairs and unlocked the basement door and descended the steps as he opened the wall and then the steel doors and entered the foul smelling confines as he returned to turn on the ventilator and returned as he looked at his captive. Her toilet was almost full as he left to put on some surgical gloves before he returned to dump her bucket. Peggy stunk from defecating and the unsanitary conditions he kept her in. he stood over her and leered at her again, the dirtier and the more she smelled the happier he was as she was now the piece of shit he believed she truly was in his sick mind. He decided to leave after sweeping up the floor and removing the paper plate and the spilled rice. Peggy was very near death as he observed the last bottle of water unopened on the floor; the small child sized toy bucket was empty and laying on its side as he observed she hadn't washed or tried to clean herself, he didn't care and started making plans to dispose of her body if she expired anytime soon. He didn't want to be found with a corpse even though the thought thrilled him.

As the days dragged on, Roger and Susan were now truly inseparable, more now than at any time in their lives as they remained at each other's side twenty-four hours a day. Besides their love for one another this was the most devastating thing to ever happen to either one as they reassured one another of their undying commitment to one another. Both missed Peggy as then held one another and cried together, Peggy had become one of them as they felt the pain of her ordeal whatever, and wherever she was and missed her very, very much. They had to remain strong for the children if nothing else. Their parents gave them strength and reassured both she would be found. Roger and Susan just wondered if she would be alive when they did.

Peggy sat in a stupor as the days dragged on, the lights never went out as she lost track on the days and hours as she seemed to sleep most of the time as she figured out the rice was heavily drugged, but had no choice as it eventually came to her who was keeping her here. Samuel J. Wine was her jailor and this was retribution for her leaving and her rebuffing his sexual harassment of her. She prayed now more than ever before and knew Susan and Roger would do all they could to find her and it's what help her maintain her sanity even as she began to feel physically weaker, and could tell she was quickly losing weight. She thought about her children and the wonderful times they enjoyed together.

It was going into week two of the kidnapping of Peggy White, no ransom note was ever received, and the observation of the most likely suspect had yield nothing as it was reported on the nightly news as Samuel Wine watched. Later a short in depth report was done describing the vibrant life and times of Peggy White and her most able abilities at being one of the most successful business women around. Roger and Susan also saw the broadcast and just hoped it wasn't her epitaph.

It was now two weeks as Peggy lay out prostrate on the concrete floor barely able to move. Samuel Wine continues with his deceptive movements as he now every two days checks on Peggy. The second Sunday after her disappearance Samuel wakes up and has a bountiful breakfast and prepares another cup of rice for his basement captive. He turns on the basement lights and watch as they flicked to life as he descends the step and turns on the ventilator, opening the wall and the metal doors to the prison he has created with it now emaciated captive. He enters and finds Peggy on the floor, unmoving but still alive. He changes her toilet and returns, removes the bed frame and leaves the dirty mattress. He returns and rolls her limp body onto the mattress that is filthy with her urine, feces and blood. Her eyes open as he stares at her, her hair is matted and has lost ten maybe more pounds or more as he spits on her before leaving, again. He has brought more water and rice but has stopped mixing the sleeping pill contents. He leaves this time and figures next time he will be cleaning up and removing her body.

The investigation into Peggy White disappearance was grinding on as the body found in the river wasn't hers and neither was the one found several counties away as Detectives began reexamining all the possible evidence, which there was hardly any except for the semen on her clothes and interviewed everyone again. It also was decided to check on Samuel Wine again and decided to again observe his movements and soon picked up his movements after finding him as he worked his ride share and began watching him more closely; five different pairs of detectives were assigned to following him now. One pair was stationed outside his apartment as two sets were assigned for the evening shift. After finding him driving his ride share job and depositing his last ride for the day the male, female team didn't arouse suspicion as they followed leisurely behind in a luxury sports car as he soon arrived at the parking garage where he was going to switch autos again, they followed and after he parked driving past as the female detective got out and was able to follow him and observed him after he parked and walked down a ramp and ducked down between the cars and slipped inside the beat up minivan, staying low as he put on his facial disguise. He sat up, looking in the mirrors, before he turned all around and found the area quiet and clear. Several cars went up the ramp and one came down. The heavy undercover presence had now observed him, and soon had his license plate number as he was closely observed as he then headed out of the parking garage. He was soon followed by a different set of detectives and Sam thought he was unobserved as he drove in the direction of the house. But then decided to stop at a grocery store and picked up a six pack of beer and some snacks. He returned to the minivan as he now finished the final leg of his journey, reaching the house as he opened the gate and pulled in back. He wasn't seen as he entered the house. His location was given by a surveillance team as another was soon placed nearby where they could watch the house unobserved. The location was called in, and a property search was instituted as the property's ownership was investigated. After an in depth records search it was found that the property was in Samuel Wines mother name even though it was purchased after her death that aroused suspicion as the people in charge decided that a search warrant should be issued. Samuel Wines movements were very suspicious as a swat team was placed on standby, the chief of police and local director of the FBI were notified and once the search warrant was issued a SWAT team was assigned and began watching and took up positions for an assault, taking note of the outside security cameras mounted all around the house. Back at headquarters an in depth property records search was instituted and all that was hidden would soon be revealed by morning.

Chapter Twenty

It had now been two very long weeks now for the White family; Roger and Susan just sat and held one another crying at times. Susan told Roger she really thought she was strong until now, but had never faced the possibility of losing a close loved one ever before, and especially Peggy, this was a stab in the heart for Susan. Roger stopped talking and drank himself to sleep some nights. Mr. White and Anne were heart broken, as were Peggy's parents. A prayer service was held for her safe return at the church where she was married after the first week that had yield no results, Roger and Susan attended as did Roger and Ethel Anne along with Bob and Sarah Thomas. All prayed they wouldn't have to return for her funeral service.

Peggy had awaken earlier, her will to live gave her the greatest strength of all and felt inside that Samuel Wine wasn't smart enough to keep her from being found, she knew the rice was drugged as it came to her in a dream who the sick and demented person was who holding her here hostage was as she remembered the voice now, and the thought frightened her now more than before after she figured it out. He was a detestable person even when she worked at Harbor. She drank as much of the water from the small toy bucket as she possibly could even though it was meant for her to bath with before she actually did start passing the damp rag over her now dry and smelly skin and trying hard to remain calm. She had done the best she could do to stay as clean as possible and maintain her sense of sanity. She ate the rice only after drinking and washing, and knew one thing about the rice was she would soon sleep. She now sat on the floor as the bed frame was now gone leaving the mattress soiled with her own feces, urine and menstrual blood as she felt very weak and knew she had lost some weight as she ate a couple more hand full of the highly drugged rice before she lay down and waited for the sleep to come over her, as she thought about her beautiful children, Susan and Roger and dreamed of being at home in their loving arms as her breathing now became shallow.

The police now had surrounded the house at 1212 NE Apple Grove St, which had been a suburb before it was merged into the city proper, but had still kept its street numbering system because it was across a small river and near a forest preserve and cemetery in what was now a very secluded part of the sprawling city. The search warrant had been issued after a records search of the property as well as department of motor vehicles and postal records indicated Samuel J Wine was the property's real owner and a in depth investigation of his past at Harbor and Associates revealed his possible lust for some type of retribution. Several teams of SWAT officers were assembled and quickly approached the front and rear entrances, they knocked on the front door, it was nine pm. A voice from inside asked, who was it, and was promptly informed it was the police and to open up. Samuel Wine panicked taking a second too long as police used hand held battering rams to enter the front and back doors at the very same time. After entering they quickly cuffed and subdued their prime suspect. They asked him where was she, he replied, where was who. Brown and Abif entered after the SWAT team and were soon directed toward the basement as the heavy metal cellar doors were opened from the outside. The basement was flooded with light and after a thorough search it was noted the paper plates in the trash can with some of the cooked rice inside, it was taken to be checked in as possible evidence. After a though search Jack said to Yansie, something isn't quite right here, as they called in the evidence technicians and told them to do a thorough search. About thirty minutes later, the senior evidence tech, Robert Walsh who knew something about the area and neighborhoods history, and about how in the early fifties and sixties people in and around this area built bomb shelters, and the neighborhood was a hotbed and the center of activity for some extreme survivalist groups of the time, and some of its past residents who probably were all deceased by now. He now began a thorough search, and one particular wall caught his interest in particular because it was almost too perfect to be in this particular house and seemed very much out of place, he soon found what he was looking for after finding the six foot long hair line almost invisible horizontal crack about an inch above the floor and followed it until it intersected with a very fine and difficult to see vertical line that resembled a crack, he pushed against one side of the wall hard, then suddenly it opened slightly as he had triggered the hidden lock for the secret wall panel, he pulled it back and opened it enough to reveal a hallway and then fully opened it. He walked to the heavy metal door down the short corridor. He pulled and slid the heavy metal bar back on the first metal door, opening the metal door and was almost immediately overwhelmed by the smell of stench, it was the overwhelming odor of human waste, and saw the nude chained body of a beautiful woman on the worn and dirty mattress on the basement floor, as he approached the heavily sedated Peggy White, with the heavy metal collar and chain around her neck. Right behind him was Jack and Yansie, as they approached and thought she was dead, her breathing was so shallow, but soon realized she was still alive and covered her with a jacket as they called for the medical technicians who had accompanied the go-team. Peggy White had been found alive as the medics, who had been waiting outside administered first aid, and covering her nude body now with a thermal blanket, as they hurriedly removed from her from the prison after the lock was cut and the collar removed from her neck and took her to the nearest hospital. The family was immediately notified that she had been found, alive as they all prepared and rushed to the hospital.

Samuel J. Wine was now under arrest and was on his way to jail for kidnapping as all he had ever touched was now under investigation. He was charged with kidnapping, attempted murder, assault, false imprisonment, evading police and a dozen other felony charges. Very soon the news broke and Jane Smithers of WXYZ and her camera crew were the first on the scene, since this was the biggest local story of the past two weeks, as the entire city was relieved that Peggy White had been found alive, and apparently unharmed as the life of Samuel J Wine and his story of retribution and hate became local and then soon national news. Thanks were given to the police and FBI for their diligence at tracking down and apprehending the culprit. His entire life history soon became public, as former associates, employees and even his ex-wife all became the center of attention and giving interviews for several days after as he was fully investigated by authorities and also the press. He was quickly brought before a judge and charged with numerous felony charges, and bail was of course denied. He was held in isolation at the city jail as he awaited arraignment and then a trial, which due to the serious circumstances would be very soon as evidence was gathered.

The entire White and Thomas families filled the small waiting room at the hospital even thought it was midnight, even little Sarah and Robert had been brought along. They were sleepy but awake, and even thought they were sleepy, Roger and Susan knew they would want to see their mother. Peggy also would want to see them also. The doctors came out and said she was very de-hydrated but would only let two people in at a time an asked that their visits be as brief as possible since she was hooked up to an intravenous drip to help restore her missing nutrients and monitors as they watched her weak vital signs. Roger and Susan were the first to enter as Peggy now awakened from her drug induced state, smiled at them as they kissed her and cried; Peggy whispered to them she knew they would soon find her. Roger left the room and next brought the children inside the room as he and Susan picked them up to kiss their mother as Peggy cried profusely. Then Roger, Susan and the children left the room as the rest of the family entered two by two. Her mother and Ethel Anne came in together and were soon followed by her father and father in-law. After everyone had visited Peggy the doctor reported she should be fully recovered in a week to ten days as they would run test to be sure she was fully recovered and nothing was seriously wrong. She had been heavily drugged with a sleeping sedative. Susan expressed the desire to stay with her while she was recovering and would sleep in the chair in her room. The doctors had no choice since Susan was very persistence as everyone else departed and Roger told Susan he would return and take her place in the morning. He kissed Peggy and Susan as he and the rest of the family members now returned home. Two uniformed police officers were also assigned to her hospital floor as a safety precaution, one was near the elevators and the other just down the hallway from her rooms door and would remain until she would be discharged, they changed shifts every eight hours and had been placed there per orders of the chief of police, and a patrol car was also posted very near the entrance of the family home as well. Besides being on the safe side it was more a show of their support for the White family.

The next morning, very early Roger returned, waking Susan and sending her home as he now sat and watched over his beloved wife. He sat and thought that he would never again allow a situation like this to ever occur again. Peggy or Susan would never again ever, be allowed to use a ride share auto and that would become a company policy, as he thought about his children also and went over the events of the past week in his mind. As a teen ager he and Susan walked around freely and went where they wanted, but were more the at home types, and weren't wild or ventured very far, so security wasn't a great concern for them, he didn't want to be over protective but would be of course more vigilant. They as a company could well afford to keep a driver or two on staff twenty four hours a day and would assign one of his top managers to handle the matter since staff did leave often for other locations on company business. He remembered Susan had a driver for her late night visits to her club locations and knew they didn't come on until late, like eight pm, and the family chauffer was really at disposal of his mother and father most of the time and with him and Susan only on special occasions. He decided he would prefer having a company driver for Peggy, Susan and the entire office staff, since they were also important in running his company and their weren't very many of them, the total number was less than twenty people. This was a very isolated incident and didn't want to over react but would act in the direction of discretion and caution. Peggy began to waken as he stood and approached her hospital bed. She opened her eyes and saw him standing there as he looked down at her smiling, tears formed in her lovely eyes as she reached weakly up to him as he bent over kissing her pretty face. When she fell asleep Susan was with her, now Roger was here when she awoke, she felt warm and loved inside as she just began crying. Roger said he loved her, as she squeezed his hand with all the strength she could muster. The morning nurse arrived and took her vitals as she spoke to her and then Roger before she departed and said the doctor would be along shortly. Ten minutes passed before two doctors came into her hospital room, they said good morning Mrs. White as they spoke to her and Roger. Then asked her how she felt, saying they wanted her out of bed today and would be giving her several test and a thorough exam, then a stress test and felt after checking her chart and vitals they might release her sooner than expected, but would really like to keep her two more days to just be on the safe side. They said she was recovering very well from her ordeal and said the nurse would be back to remove the drip and wanted her to shower and take care of her personal hygiene and said they knew her condition after the extensive emergency exam she had been given the night before. They took her breakfast order and she was to eat before she attempted to bath. They assured Roger she would receive the best of care.

Employees of ROWE, and the White Company were ecstatic at the news of Peggy White having been found, and the capture of the culprit; it was front page news in both daily newspapers and all the television stations news broadcast, with all five of the major local stations jockeying to have the most complete coverage. As a matter of fact, the entire city was relieved at Peggy being found alive; she was a well admired semipublic figure and an example for women everywhere. Susan went home and showered, ate, changed clothes and hurriedly returned to the hospital, she had slept in the comfortable chair in Peggy's room overnight with her and was very relieved she was back with them. When she arrived back at the hospital she rushed by news reporters as the small contingent of three hospital security guards and two police officers escorted her from the family limousine.

She went directly to Peggy's room and arrived as she was eating breakfast. Susan kissed her and stepped back as she smiled. She told Roger about the crush of reporters downstairs and said he should be the one to make a statement to the press. Roger kissed Peggy as she finished eating, and said he would be back later in the day, they kissed again as he departed. Soon a room orderly removed her tray and left as a nurse entered and brought her a clean gown to put on after she bathed and also said another orderly would come soon and change her bed sheets. She asked Peggy did she need any assistance to bathe. Peggy replied Susan was here with her and she should be able to manage. A weak Peggy slowly stood, and said she was starting to feel more like herself again. Her and Susan hugged and held each other as they both cried for several long minutes, kissing one another as if they had been apart for several years. Peggy entered the bathroom and Susan assisted her, she first sat on the toilet as she described how good it felt and what she had to use while in captivity, what she had to sleep on and the chain around her neck. The bruise marks from the collar had all but disappeared, as she stood and turned on the shower and waited a very short time as the water warmed up, she entered and just stood as the warm water cascaded all over her body as Susan handed her a wash cloth and a bar of soap. She bathed first then washed her dirty hair, Susan handed her the douche to use and Peggy asked for another one after using the first one. Susan looked out into the room as an orderly changed the linen and departed. Peggy said the water felt so very wonderful, as she just stood underneath before turning it off and stepped into a towel Susan held and wrapped around her, holding her as she showered her with passionate kisses again. Susan released her and gave her a towel to wrap her hair in after drying off and retrieving the hospital gown as she escorted her back into the hospital room. Peggy said she loved her, now more than ever and couldn't wait to be home between her and Roger. Soon a nurse appeared with a wheel chair in the hallway and said it was time for her stress test and brought with her a white smock to wear that covered her body much better. Peggy put it on and Susan escorted Peggy to the hallway as she sat in the chair and adjusted it. The nurse said she would be back in a couple hours and in time for lunch. Susan said she would return later with Roger as she kissed Peggy again and prepared to depart.

When Roger reached the lobby of the hospital, he prepared himself for the onslaught and crush of reporters as he called for the family limousine to pick him up. Once he saw the auto approach he exited and read from a hastily prepared statement before he answered any questions. He replied that Mrs. Peggy White was doing very well after her stressful ordeal and probably would be released in a few days or whenever the doctors felt she had recovered. They asked him about the culprit and how he felt. Roger replied it was a matter for the law, as they pressed him for his personal opinion. Roger said no comment and made his way to the limousine with the aid of hospital security and several police officers, and rode away to his office. There were matters that had been re-scheduled, and needed to be attended to since not anything of real importance was taken care of with the CFO missing.

Susan when she departed went straight to the family limousine since Roger sent it back to wait for her and she arrived at work a couple hours later. She met Roger, they hugged and held one another for a long time as they cried and kissed before they sat down and Roger informed her of his having one or two company cars for them and all office staff for official business and he wasn't prepared for a situation like this to ever occur again and would supplement the needs of the family also and now was more concerned about the children. He stated he didn't want to be over bearing but cautious about the situation. Company policy would now be, company cars only when on company business, and stated he had placed his top manager to oversee the new policy right away, as of yesterday. Susan smiled at him and suggested they go to lunch before returning to the hospital. He said there wasn't anything of importance to be accomplished until Peggy returned and since most of the important matters had been postponed until her return. They prepared to depart just as his business manager called and said the auto situation had been taken care of and had temporarily hired a livery company to be on standby twenty four seven, with two dedicated drivers on standby until he could hire and investigate the back grounds of some trustworthy people to become drivers. He was also looking into having them be ex-military or retired federal agents or police, and possibly be armed and had contacted a couple dealers about the type of vehicles he felt would be acceptable to a company of our size and reputation. Roger thanked him and said very well and would soon personally discuss the matter fully after Peggy was out of the hospital, thanking him and hung up as he and Susan departed for lunch. Roger called the manager right back and said he needed a ride now for him and Susan. He said one was waiting downstairs now, and said he would go downstairs with them if he gave him a minute. Susan and Roger waited by the elevator as his manager came running out of his office putting on his suit jacket as he approached and said, good evening Mr. White and Ms. Stone as they entered the elevator together and handed both a business card for the livery service as the doors closed and stated this was a well-respected livery service with luxury vehicles and the employees had all passed a security screening. The elevator doors opened and he led his boss to a large luxury SUV and the driver was standing with the back door open as his manager, Haskin Sims introduced him to the driver and stated he would be with him all day if need be. Roger shook the drivers hand as Susan entered the vehicle and Roger walked around to the other side as the driver opened the door for him. The vehicle was just a couple months old as the driver requested they place the phone number on the business card he handed them as he introduced himself in their cell phones, and said they needed to call if they were to stay anywhere more than half an hour because of the parking situation in the city and especially the business district. They both understood as their new driver Tony pulled away after they buckled up and Susan told him where to go.

Susan commented on the size and leg room and said this was very nice and comfortable, it sat up so much higher than the limousine and she liked the view as she looked out and commented you could see so much more. Roger took note of the make and model, before they soon arrived at their destination. Tony pulled up placing the vehicle in park as he got out and opened the door for Roger then walked around and then let Susan out. Roger informed him they would be here for an hour or maybe two, yes sir Tony replied as they walked toward the entrance of the 500 club for lunch. After entering they were immediately shown to the reserved booth as a waiter promptly appeared and handed them the menus and informed them of the special for the day, took their drink order and departed. He very quickly returned with a chilled bottle of Petite Sirah and two wine glasses and filled them half way. They ordered and sat back sipping the chilled wine as they talked and waited on their orders. As they waited on their lunch order Roger received a call from Peggy, she was using the hospital phone since the police hadn't returned her personal belonging yet, said she loved him and said she had passed the stress test and they would release her maybe sometime tomorrow. He said he and Susan were at lunch, and afterwards they would come back to see her. She said her mother and Anne with the children had just entered her room and would see him and Susan later.

The children adored their mother as she held them both as they sat on the edge of the bed and little Robert clung to her; Sarah hugged her and asked where had mommy been and wanted her to come home. She released them as her mother Sarah kissed her, and said she was glad she was doing well. Peggy told them she might be released tomorrow, as Ethel Anne said very well as they spent more than an hour with her. After the family had left, shortly after a couple of city detectives and two federal agents came to her room. They had a bag with them, and inside was her phone, jewelry, purse, wallet and her shoes. She thanked them and they asked her if she would mind answering a few questions. Peggy said she would be more than happy to. They asked her if she had ever seen or recognized him before being picked up that day or any time before. She said no because she had a busy schedule and very happy life and really didn't pay much attention to the ride share drivers, and said she had a couple who had driven her more than once. After getting in the car, did she recognize him, his appearance or voice in any way? She said no because she was using her phone at the time and it was and unusually busy day for her as she was going to check the new coolers at the warehouse and seldom looked up until when he stopped suddenly, then surprised her when he jumped in the back seat with her, and held the rag over her face and when she awoke again she was laying naked and chained, having no clue where she was and began to panic when she realized her wedding ring and earrings were gone as she looked around the bare room. They asked her about the rice and if she knew it was drugged. She replied after eating it the second time, she knew it was then because it tasted bitter and always put her to sleep. They asked her if he assaulted her in any way. Said she didn't think so, it was her time of the month and any blood they found was probably hers and menstrual. They apologized for her having to go through such an ordeal and thanked her and said they would possibly talk to her again at a later date. They departed and the day had been very trying on her as she lay down, looking out the window and dosed off to sleep. When she woke again Susan was holding her hand as Roger sat in the chair looking at her. She smiled and then a cheerful orderly entered and said time to eat my dear as he cleared her tray table before he went back into the hallway for her dinner tray. They feed her very well here and she had a bountiful amount of food on her tray. Peggy soon consumed it all and belched when she finished as Roger laughed and said she's back. Peggy felt so much better and told them to go home as she turned the television on and looked at them both and said you both look very tired. She told them she wanted them fresh and happy whenever they came to get her and said the police will be here until she is released and she would be ok. They relented, kissing her and Susan asked her what clothes did she want, she wrote it down and handed it to Susan and gave her the jewelry that had been returned except her wedding and engagement rings, Roger placed it on her hand again as they kissed one another. Peggy said she would keep her purse after she had gone through it and found all of her personal items and credit cards. Told Susan she would keep her shoes and handed her a list. They hugged and kissed each other as Roger and Susan departed. Peggy sat up in the bed and watched some television and saw herself on the late news before she turned it off and soon went to sleep.

Chapter Twenty One

The two days later on Sunday, Peggy was to be released as Roger and Susan came to her hospital room; she had eaten breakfast and was taking a warm shower when they entered. Susan knocked on the bathroom door as Peggy peeped out and then let her inside. Roger was sitting in the lounge chair as he heard laughter and felt better knowing she was herself again. Peggy put the hospital clothes on the bed since the doctors had been around early and had signed her release. She just had to wait on the hospital staff to come and take her downstairs in a wheelchair as was the customary hospital policy. Susan had followed Peggy's instructions and brought her the simple one piece beige dress with a matching jacket, the blue purse and shoes went well with it. She just wore some stud earrings and her charm bracelet.

The nurse soon appeared and the police officers were to accompany her as she departed because their detail would end when she departed the hospital grounds. Peggy entered the hallway and sat in the wheel chair as the nurse adjusted it, then the small entourage made its way downstairs. Once she had exited the hospital to an excited throng of newspaper and television reporters who security held back, Peggy stood turned and thanked the nurse as she just waved as she then entered the waiting livery Roger had hired. Peggy and Susan sat together as Roger sat up front with the driver and having a police escort as they departed. It wasn't long before they arrived back home; Tony the driver opened the car doors for them as they entered the main lobby entrance, and the doorman greeted her as he held the door open as she entered, building staff who saw her enter applauded, as she shook their hands and thanked them before her and Roger along with Susan took their private elevator up to their home. As they exited the elevator Roger Sr. and Ethel and the children along with her parents were waiting and welcomed her home, along with all the household staff from both houses. Peggy couldn't hold back the tears as she held her children's hands and hugged each one. Ethel Anne led them inside as she had lunch prepared that Susan had catered as they all sat down together and Roger Sr. said a prayer, thanking god for Peggy's safe return.

Later that afternoon after everyone had slowly took their time departing and Peggy's parents and close relatives also went home, things began to return back to a semblance of normality, as the children along with Roger, Peggy and Susan returned next door where they relaxed somewhat as Peggy said she wanted a nice stiff drink. After they all had one, they hugged her as they all cried as they held one another again. Soon Roger and Susan were all in Peggy's large shower, standing nude as they caressed one another as Peggy and Roger made love and Susan caressed them both. Peggy said she had missed being with both of them, and especially like this as they continued kissing. They enjoyed each other sexually as Peggy and Susan had multiple climaxes, then Roger came, as they washed and once again enjoyed being together. They dried and oiled one another then sat hugging and massaging Peggy as Roger fixed her favorite drink. Roger said to her that never again would she take a ride share and explained to her what he had instituted and what was now there new company policy. Peggy hugged him and cried and kissed him. After a number of drinks they all were well out of it as they headed to bed and snuggled up together in Susan's bed, it's where she wanted to sleep.

Peggy spent a restful weekend at home with Roger and Susan and made it known she was more than thankful for all their attention and concern, but she really wanted to return to work. Said she was thankful no serious harm had come to her either mentally or physically. Monday morning they as a group returned to work and Peggy resumed her regular duties and said tomorrow being Tuesday she would go to the warehouse as she had originally planned to do. As lunch time rolled around the three of them went together, and Peggy was now introduced to the livery driver, Tony. She also commented about the SUV they were riding in just as Susan had the week before. They arrived at the restaurant, this time going to the Silver Club where they would have lunch. Peggy said she liked the idea of having a company car and said they could well afford it, and it was a business expense any way. They enjoyed a bountiful lunch and then returned back to ROWE headquarters. All the business that had been postponed and had been rescheduled was soon being cleared up as Peggy resumed her most important duties. After a day at work when she was joined by Susan, said she felt really good now. Susan hadn't asked her anything about her ordeal and asked if she ever wanted to talk about it she was here. Peggy thanked her for her concern as she stood and came from behind her desk and they hugged and kissed. Peggy said it made her appreciate every little thing in life a lot more now and not to take anything for granted. Said it did give her some ideas as she looked back on the experience.

Roger had contacted an attorney and wanted to proceed with a civil suit against Samuel J Wine for damages, the attorney said he would happily take the case. Soon it was time to call it a day as they all gathered in Rogers's office and then headed home. They arrived and Peggy wanted to stop at the hair salon on the mezzanine, one she used on a regular basis and had called earlier and made an appointment as she visited her regular hair stylist. Susan went in with her and waited with her until her stylist finished with another customer before calling Peggy. Peggy asked Susan to please stay with her; she did and read a magazine since Peggy was only getting a cut and trim. She was there only a half hour before they went upstairs together. When they entered and went to their bed rooms Peggy stopped, took Susan's hand pulled her to the side and asked her to make love to her. It wasn't long before both were in Susan's bed as they engaged in making passionate love to one another again, something they both had missed very much. After and exhausting session, they dressed in there lounging clothes and joined Roger and the children downstairs for dinner. The children were happy and playful as usual and had started school earlier in the year and were progressing very well. After dinner the au pair took the children to their rooms and would later bathe them and put them in bed and soon they would be asleep. Later that evening Roger said good night ladies, kissed them both and went to their bed room and was asleep in no time, the past week had taken a heavy mental toll on him and he was just now catching up with his rest as his ever expanding empire had him handing more responsibilities to his slowly growing staff of trusted employees. He now was in the process of designating more responsibilities to others. He had talked to Susan and Peggy about it also, and they also agreed with him, but there were somethings Peggy just wouldn't stop doing, and that was her almost weekly inspection of the food warehouse operations. Peggy and Susan sat up a little longer as she began to tell Susan how it felt being chained like a dog and having to smell your own excrement and urine all day, and about the thoughts she had as she laid on the dirty floor and dirty mattress. Said it made her more appreciative of the small everyday things, like when you wanted some cold water, or have a snack, and seeing and hearing the people you love. And how she had prayed and was very thankful she wasn't physically harmed or abused, which she feared might happen at any time. How she ate the rice even when she knew it was drugged, because she dreamed of being in bed with her and Roger, and the sound of the children who she really missed and prayed she would survive to see them all again, said it was a very humbling experience. Susan hugged her again as they stood and went where Roger was sleeping, undressed and climbed in bed besides him, and very soon they were asleep also.

The following day, Tuesday, Peggy was at her desk for an hour before setting out for the food distribution warehouse and Susan said she would accompany her this time. She went to Susan's office and said lets go sister. Susan looked up and stood and they went downstairs together and walked across the vast lobby to the waiting SUV. Mr. Tony opened the door for them as they stepped inside. There was an area in front where he and another available SUV waited on standby for only ROWE employees. Tony had been given a list of various company locations, including all the buildings and restaurants. He was a very careful driver, an ex-military policeman, and also was armed. Roger knew, but Peggy and Susan didn't, since Roger didn't want to make them feel paranoid, but wanted them safe. Roger through his manager found out about the livery service and the drivers, it was a small outfit, three ex-military policemen who had started there protective livery service for hire and were doing very well and Roger was prepared to hire all three, or rather the entire company. After a couple of weeks Roger had his manager make an offer to the livery service, it was a very lucrative offer. They could remain independent with a long term contract, or become employees, and the offer was negotiable. Soon Roger had a meeting with all three men together. He liked them and they accepted the offer Roger made, to remain independent contractors, but exclusive to ROWE and also the White company, and the White family. It was a very over lapping deal since they would be covered by the company's health insurance as employees. They would now provide twenty four hour coverage and Susan's two security drivers agreed and were accepted by the livery company and would also be included so there would be full availability now with five people providing security. It was a good deal for Roger, he now had a small private and very experienced personal security force, or service at his disposal. It became something he would later pursue and expand on.

Peggy accompanied by Susan, soon arrived at the warehouse. When she entered, and the employees saw her they cheered and applauded, most came and personally greeted her since she just about knew each one by name. She and Susan went to see the new coolers; after she put on a heavy insulated coat as did the manager, Albert Pain, as her and Susan were given a guided tour of the large state of the art food coolers. She even inspected the one for just frozen foods very briefly. The cold section now took up half the building. The manager showed her the new flow chart for the way he had changed the way they operated and said it saved a whole day in sorting out the needed items and had speedup delivery times. Additional backup generators had also been installed as Peggy and Susan looked at the state of the art instillation. Peggy said she was more than satisfied by the new operation. Albert said that all the employees had held a prayer vigil for her and were over joyed when she was found alive. She thanked him as he escorted her and Susan to the waiting SUV. Susan told her on the ride back the entire city had prayed for her and they even had a service at the church. Peggy began to get teary eyed as Susan reached out and held her hand, and said she loved her very, very much. Susan suggested they have an early lunch since the bank representative was scheduled to return to present again the presentation that was terminated the day she disappeared. Peggy said that was a good idea as they headed to the Uptown Club as she informed the driver. Peggy said it has been a long time since we were there last; it was one brand they had yet to expand on. It had a pleasant no frills atmosphere but the food was exceptional, the décor was art deco and occupied a space that had been a restaurant for several decades. When Roger bought the building, the restaurant had been closed for several years, which was unusual for the vibrant neighborhood it was in. But after Roger purchased the building he understood why as he had the building undergo a major renovation and upgraded everything from the heating system, elevators and especially the restaurant with its obsolete out of date kitchen. He kept the restaurant seating areas as much in tack as possible salvaging the ornate art deco fixtures and wood work and having it completely refurbished and reinstalled and now it was a very beautiful one of a kind place to dine and had gained a reputation all its own from several of the top restaurant critics. He and Susan said they liked the art deco and he spared no expense with its restoration and moderation, it all came together nicely when it was finished. Susan had a reserved and very plush booth; it was cleaned every day and was even roped off. When they entered, the maître, lead them directly to their table, it was about eleven thirty as they were getting ready for the lunch crowd. This wasn't an inexpensive place to eat; caviar was even on the menu, as well as other very select offerings not found else ware even in their other restaurants. The waiter took their drink order and when he returned Peggy ordered the steak and lobster as Susan ordered the broiled salmon.

They sat and talked as they were observed by a famous restaurant critic from one of the major newspapers. They enjoyed their lunch and the reporter was close behind as they departed and made note of the SUV and the no frills driver. Peggy wasn't riding in ride shares any longer; it was very obvious now to anyone who observed her movements.

That afternoon the bank representative returned. To again present to Susan and now Peggy a new proposal for her dinners and club card operation. Roger soon attended the meeting as this was going to present them supposedly with a very new and possibly lucrative venture and turn the card more into a credit card but based on their reputation. The bank had observed the usage rates and wanted to exploit the cards very good reputation, but wanted to charge interest on the unpaid balances. Just as before Susan said the full board would have to accept the proposal first, as he finished up his presentation. Susan said they would discuss it further and give him a decision very soon before the end of the week. He departed as Susan and Roger said we would be giving up full control if we accept this offer from the bank. Peggy said she didn't like it and it would destroy the good will of our loyal customers. Both Susan and Roger agreed with her and decided they would wait several days before they gave the bank there reply. Peggy said we have our own card department and it is functioning at a lower cost than what he claimed it would cost them to handle the transactions for us. Susan said, screw them and they left the conference room together. Peggy at Susan's suggestion said lets go upstairs and walk around, then go home, she said ok. They visited the card department and went back to clear their desk and headed home but decided to go shopping first. The two of them spent a couple hours as they purchased some perfumes and other small item before they decided to head home.

When they arrived home Peggy remarked she hadn't heard any bells lately, Susan laughed, said she hadn't heard any either. They went together to find Min, and soon found her sitting in her room. They had her follow them upstairs to Susan's bedroom where they made her undress as they found the bells were still in place, they checked her piercings. The small bells had soap film inside and weren't as loud as they once were. Susan wasn't happy with the situation; and decided on removing the bells and would have Marie clean them as she began to carefully removing the small bells and then undressed and made Min service her and then Peggy as they hugged and kissed. When they were satisfied they took Min to the bathroom and had her bath them both. When they were finished they dismissed Min as they dressed and waited on Roger to come home and had a drink as they waited. Peggy told Susan she was getting ideas on how to truly terrify someone after her ordeal. Said it was a very dark place in her mind and hoped it would soon pass from her thoughts. Susan hugged her and told her not to dwell on the negative, but the positive in her life and even suggested maybe she should see a therapist. Peggy said it would pass; it was her inner self that probably wanted some type of satisfaction. After Roger came home they all went to dinner with the children as usual before retiring for the evening and pursuing their usual routine. Peggy was sitting quietly in the living room, she had thoughts about her ordeal that hadn't happened, the perverse thoughts that excited her very much as Susan sat next to her and asked her what was she thinking about. The television wasn't on as she just sat looking out the large picture window. She told Susan that she wanted her and Roger to take her to the play room, and described in detail what she wanted them to do to her, and specifically how she wanted it done, and for how long. Susan then asked why, and Peggy answered she couldn't explain why, but said she was turned on when she thought about the ordeal and wanted to experience it again with her and Roger in control of the situation because they loved her and she wouldn't be harmed and would feel safe. Susan asked her how soon she wanted this to occur, and Peggy replied very soon, please. Susan kissed and hugged her tight and said it isn't necessary or normal to want to experience it again as Peggy turned to her, her eyes moist and almost in tears, said please sister, would you do as I ask, and said she knew her and Roger would be reluctant to fulfill her request . Susan stood and took Peggy's hand as she also stood and hugged her tight and said she loved her very much and asked her to please reconsider, Peggy looked at her and said if you really love me then you need to do as I ask, as Peggy kissed Susan passionately as they went together and joined Roger in bed.

Chapter Twenty Two

The day started as a normal work day for everyone as usual, it was a Friday and Peggy told Susan she wanted to do a half day at work before they would leave to fulfill her special request. Susan along with Roger and Peggy went to lunch together, this time to the Executive Club and were promptly seated in there reserved booth. They sat and ate a beautiful lunch; Peggy knew it would be her last decent meal for the next couple of days, per her request to Roger and Susan. Roger had listened to Susan describe Peggy's request that she asked them to fulfill and had taken the time to have the walk in closet just off the playroom prepared to fulfill the special request that Peggy was asking them to do to her. Peggy had also spoken to Roger about it and begged him as he first told her he wouldn't do it as she even got down on her knees and begged as she cried, he still refused. She again asked him and Susan together and stated it was some unknown, unfulfilled need she had to satisfy. He had the building maintenance staff install the required hooks in the walls and ceiling. Roger didn't know if he really was looking forward to fulfilling Peggy's perverse request; it wasn't too much different from what they had already done to her in the past, except Peggy wanted this to last a couple days and was similar to her recent kidnapping experience. After lunch they returned to work for a short period of time, as Susan called and arraigned for Min to be brought to Sutton place at a designated time later that same day. Min would be needed to clean up the premises. After spending time wrapping up there business affairs for the next few days and informing there management staff to take charge, at least until the middle of next week they headed as a group to Sutton place and soon after arriving headed upstairs to the penthouse, playhouse. After entering Peggy turned to Roger and Susan and asked them not to spare her, and not to have any mercy on her, and also requested them to leave her chained and in her own filth and to take full advantage of her if they truly loved her. Said that she would be safe with them but something unknown was inside of her driving her to experience this perverted humiliation again. Peggy had written down exactly what she wanted done to her, as she began to undressed and removed all of her clothing and jewelry, and requested that they show her no affection, mercy or compassion and do whatever they wanted for the requested time she designated.

Roger kissed her passionately with tears in his eyes, telling her he really loved her very, very much and only because she was requesting this to be done as he held her kissing her and was the only reason he would do it before he led her into the dark room, it was originally designed to be a large walk-in closet but was just four bare walls that had been painted in a high gloss washable black paint with the baseboards sealed tight to prevent any liquids from seeping out, a sturdy hook had been attached near center of the ceiling, and a long sturdy grey plastic chain that hung from it and was several feet long as some of it lay on the floor and a metal collar was attached at its very end. Roger attached the collar to his beloved wife's neck, kissed her, turned and left the room, locking the door. A camera had been installed inside as Susan went and turned on a laptop and observed Peggy. Peggy wanted to be abused and used. Roger and Susan went and changed clothes, putting on some leather pants and vest, then gathering some cuffs, whips, chains and dildos. They returned to the room, entered and spoke to Peggy in the most degrading manner they could, telling her to stand up bitch. She stood as they placed a dark hood over her head and shortened the chain attached to her neck taking the slack out and forcing her to stand as they cuffed both wrist and attached a chain to each, then attaching them to the walls as Peggy was stretched out from wall to wall. Roger touched her as her knees bent slightly and Susan then attached cuffs to her ankles, before attaching a spreader bar, spreading Peggy as wide open as possible. Roger left and returned with a large anal plug and placed some lubricant on her anus as he roughly inserted several fingers of his now gloved hand inside of her before he inserted the large anal plug inside his wife's anus as she moaned. They looked at her and departed the room, as they went and fixed a drink. They watched the computer screen as Peggy was stretched out, and Roger said time to fulfill her request as they returned. He removed the hood and placed a blind fold over her eyes. Roger whispered in her ear, you know why you are hear, she replied yes sir master. He then placed a ball gag in her mouth as he put some slack in the chain attached to her neck collar. Susan handed him the flogger then stepped back as Roger began using it on her as she jerked and shook with each blow as Roger spared no part of her body before handing it over to Susan's expert hands. Susan was an expert with whips and decided to use a riding crop after several hard strikes with the whip on

Peggy. Susan enjoyed the pain she inflicted on Peggy and especially now in her moment of self-depredation. She really and truly loved her very much, but deep inside never wanted to really share Roger with anyone, and that thought would now allow her to take full advantage of Peggy's painful and subverted wishes. Susan could inflict exquisite, precise and very intense pain as she knew all of a female's very sensitive anatomy more so than many men, even doctors as she watched Peggy flinch violently with ever strike. Susan finished, as Roger then attached a harness around Peggy's waist, and brought it up between her legs the portion with a cruel looking short dildo with little short hard rounded fingers as he slowly inserted it into her now very wet and swollen crotch and attached it securely in front. When they finished they again left the room. They went and sipped their drinks and when they finished went to the bedroom where they made love. Susan told Roger, she really never wanted to share him with anyone and he said he never really wanted anyone but her until Peggy came into both their lives. They both agreed that having Peggy in their lives turned out to be a bonus. They loved her and each other deeply and very soon fell asleep in each other's arms.

It was close to midnight when Roger woke to use the bathroom; he looked at Susan and returned as she was awaken. She stood and they hugged as she went to the bathroom and returned, they put on some robes and checked the laptop and looked as they watched Peggy, they could tell she was very uncomfortable, and decided it was time to remove the harness and the anal plug and again leave her. When they entered Roger removed the harness, followed by the anal plug along with the ball gag and just as they stepped away reaching the door, Peggy let go of her bowels, as she defecated and urinated, and they quickly closed the door. Susan said based on her request to them, she wanted to be degraded and abused and they would gladly and definitely help her fulfill her perverted wish. They returned to the bedroom and slept until early morning. After waking and having washed and relieved themselves, decided to check on Peggy as they checked the room. Min was in her room after arriving the evening before and letting herself in as she had done many times when she came to clean up. They woke her up, instructing her to go prepare breakfast. They went and checked on Peggy, she was hanging limply, her outstretched arms held her up and in place, her head hung down and her knees were bent, there were whelps all over her shapely body along with red bruises, the room reeked from her losing control of her bowels as Roger removed the blindfold and she opened her eyes. They removed the spreader bar and cuffs, the collar from her neck, and then Roger held her as Susan removed the cuffs from her wrist. Roger then laid her on the floor in her own excrement as they departed with the cuffs and bar. They left her there for several more hours as they watched her wallow and defecate again before they went, and carried her to a shower in a nearby bathroom. They bathed her and they took full advantage of her sexually. Peggy climaxed several times and begged them not to stop. They dried her off, oiled her and then placed a leather dog collar on her neck and a leash and made her crawl as they led her around like a dog. Roger ordered

Min to clean the room Peggy had been kept in and gave her a small wet dry vacuum to use. Roger and Susan took Peggy to the play room and place her in the chair Min had been placed in when they pierced her. They strapped Peggy in the chair as she fell asleep now going a step further than she had requested as they secured her in the chair. Roger washed and cleaned Peggy's vagina again after putting on his surgical gloves and spreading her wide open as he proceeded to clamp her labia, Susan handed him the large piercing needle and the rings as she had a big wide grin on her face. Roger soon completed the task and used small rings but large enough to place a padlock on. They woke Peggy up before they released her and then led her around after placing handcuffs on her arms behind her back. They led her around and back to the play room, released her hands and placed her in a cage that was a four foot cube with bars on five sides. Peggy hadn't eaten since yesterday and the only water she had drunk was when she was in the shower. They left the room as Peggy began crying after she found they had pierced her vagina. They returned a couple hours later, let her out as she stood and led her over and cuffed her hands in front and raised them up and attached them to a bar above her head. Peggy begged and pleaded for mercy now, Roger slapped her a couple times and said this is what you wanted bitch, and that's what you are going to get; the way he said it truly frightened her. And then reminded her they were only following her strict orders, as she cried and said she changed her mind, he told that was too bad bitch, it was too late and besides she was his to do with whatever he wanted. He took a square metal bar, four inches square and three feet long and attached a chain to one end and then placed it between her legs as he then attached the other end to another chain as it pressed deeply inside of Peggy between her thighs and between the rings he had just attached, he bent down tied a small chain to one ring and around the bar to the other, tying it securely as it pulled on her vaginal lips and her body weight pressed her against the bar as she was standing on her tip toes as she strained to hold herself up. Susan looked on smiling with a wicked grin. Then Susan approached and attached a large pair of binder clips to each of her now very swollen nipples as she screamed loudly from the intense pain.

Roger then kissed her and said careful what you ask for slut, as they departed the room. After an hour and having eaten lunch they returned to find Peggy crying profusely as she looked up at them and begged for mercy. They released her removing her bonds except for the collar and leash and returned her to the closet as they made her crawl. Min had done an excellent job cleaning the room as they led her inside again. Peggy pleaded with them that she had enough. Roger and Susan decided to relent and made her stand. Roger held her head up and said they would change up some from her request but she would still have to spend the entire weekend just as she had requested. He said she was a slave and would serve them as they saw fit and to address them as master and mistress. Peggy said she understood as they made her crawl and Susan went to the room and returned with two dog dishes which they placed some food in one and water in the other as they allowed her to eat on her hands and knees like a dog. They sat and watched and made snide remarks as they watched her. Peggy felt total humiliation now as she finished eating and was then made to lick Rogers's boots, then was told to lick Susan shoes as he pressed the toe of his boot in her vagina causing her to climax, then having to lick them clean. They let her use the bathroom before they locked her in the cage again leaving her there for several more hours before they returned and let her out to entertain them and having Min undress and ride her like a horse. They laughed as they watched her total humiliation and degradation. They made her service Min and lick her ass before telling Min to clean up as they led her to the closet as she pleaded with them as they placed the collar around her neck and left her there for the night, instructing her to use the bed pan if need be, and if she didn't she would be punished as they laughed. This internal hell was of Peggy's own making, she was a submissive and inside her mind she needed to be subjected to punishment to function. Roger and Susan had always been her master and mistress and she could trust them as she sat and thought about her request and they had fulfilled it superbly, she never expected to be pierced as she felt the rings and played with them and herself as she stretched out on the bare tile floor and fingered herself, soon having a massive and most intense climax before she stretched out and went to sleep.

Roger and Susan watched her now on the television as she climaxed and played with herself as they had drinks and commented as they watched her and listened to her through the speakers. Susan asked Roger what he thought was driving her to be this way. Roger said you should know better than me since she was like this when we first met her, remember when you pointed her out to me. She is a true and natural submissive and probably was looking to be abused when she was held captive and she feels unfulfilled. Susan said I believe you are so right. Roger stated he had observed other women and some men who had a need to be submissive and abused or even masochistic to function and there were several internet sites that catered to people like her and you could watch them as they had their desires fulfilled and said we just have one all to ourselves in Peggy. He said tomorrow we will see how she feels, said she wouldn't even tell you what we did this weekend when you talk to her. Roger reminded Susan, you know this wasn't the first time she asked us to do this to her. Susan said I am glad she is like this, and said the only reason we didn't humiliate her in public was because she is your wife and CFO. Roger said thank you as they kissed and turned the television off and went to bed.

The next morning after waking Roger and Susan hugged one another and said let's freshen up and see what condition Peggy's in. They opened the door and found her lying on the floor. Roger removed the collar as she turned over and sat up reaching out and hugging him and kissing him passionately. He stood and helped her to her feet as she stepped over to Susan and they hugged. The room was clean as he released her, and then led her to the bathroom to clean and shower. Peggy came out of the bathroom as Susan and Roger massaged and oiled her body, she was one very pretty and shapely woman and soon they all dressed up and went to eat breakfast. Min had just finished as they sat down and ate together including Min. Afterwards Roger took Min and showed her what he wanted cleaned up. Susan took Peggy to the enclosed terrace as they sat and talked and Peggy thanked her and Roger for fulfilling her special request and said she felt so much better now. Roger returned as they all now talked and Peggy said she felt really exhilarated and could accomplish anything as Roger hugged her. Peggy said she was ready to return home after they made love to her. They all went to the bedroom and engaged in some serious and sensuous sex. Roger and Susan used Peggy to the fullest as she enjoyed being subject to their perverted ways. Several hours later they returned home together with Min as Roger drove one of the family cars he kept here. Everyone returned to work the following Wednesday after resting Tuesday and Peggy seamed more full of energy and more driven as her and Susan spent a couple days inspecting some of the far flung suburban restaurant locations and spending a several nights away from home in some exclusive hotels. She was her sweet self again and showed no signs of her weekend ordeal. She did ask Roger one night to spank her with a belt which wasn't unusual before he made love to her which was a real turn on for her. He and Susan felt she had freed herself of what ever had bothered her and left it at that, an never ever questioned her about it or any of her request, she was their sweet Peggy and it was just how she was.

Chapter Twenty Three

More than fifteen months had passed since the kidnapping of Mrs. Peggy White before the trial of Samuel J. Wine was to begin in state court, since he hadn't taken her across any state lines; the state took charge of the case as he was looking at several serious felony charges. Peggy didn't have to attend the trial, since he had admitted to her abduction. The trial only lasted two days and was a bench trial where he was sentenced to life in prison without the possibility of parole. Rogers's civil suit progressed swiftly through the court system afterwards and Samuel J. Wine's property was the only thing of value he had and Roger took possession of the property and the lawsuit against him was then settled. Roger a couple months after winning his civil suit accompanied by his driver an Susan meet one of the police detectives who was assigned to the kidnapping case when it was active meeting him at the property location, 1212 Apple Grove St. The property still had some police tape around some portions of the house and seals on the doors as they entered the premises as Roger and Susan looked around inside of every room before they went downstairs to the basement and detective Yansie Brown showed Roger the hidden wall and the place where Peggy had been held, they looked around and took photos of the small space and the house with his cell phone, and both he and Susan soon said they had seen enough as they exited the house. Detective Brown asked Roger what he might do with the property, and Roger replied he didn't know yet, and thanked him for showing him around, shaking hands before they all departed. On the ride back, Roger and Susan agreed it was a very dismal place and said they had a better understanding now about the weekend Peggy had requested of them. They now had pictures and would see dear Peggy very soon since they didn't even tell her where they had gone; as a matter of fact it was Tuesday and she had gone to the warehouse.

They arrived back at ROWE headquarters, and returned with Susan coming to his office as his phone sent the pictures automatically to his computer; soon Susan could view them on the large screen. Neither of them had forgotten about that weekend several month back when Peggy had requested them to abuse her in the closet causing them both to watch her a little more closely afterwards. Susan skimmed through the photos and was truly intrigued by the room Peggy had been kept in even though she had went with Roger. Susan remarked it was similar to the closet, but much cruder, and much more humiliating. Roger said yes and asked her not to tell Peggy about their visit or the photos, and said he had instructed the driver not to say or mention anything to Peggy either. Peggy could be very talkative sometimes when she was driven around and both had been keeping a close eye on her ever since out of a real concern for her mental health and state of mind even though she didn't exhibit any signs of being unstable. There weeks later Peggy found out about Roger winning the civil suit against Samuel J Wine and in a casual conversation while lounging at home asked Roger what he had gotten out of the lawsuit, Peggy knew the answer before she even asked, she just wanted to see if Roger was going to be truthful with her and say anything. He did and told her he had acquired possession of the house she had been held in and was looking to purchase additional property around it in the neighborhood and possibly build a new housing development for low income people in the area. Roger hadn't mentioned it because he was afraid she might want to see it again and didn't know what might happen if she did, but one thing he didn't do was lie to his wife or Susan, ever. Peggy said that was a wonderful idea, she looked him in his eyes and said, she knew why he hadn't mentioned anything to her about it because he was afraid it would bring back memories of what had happened to her and said after her special request she knew Susan and him were keeping a close eye on her. He said yes, they were, because they loved her so very much. She came over and climbed into his lap and placed her arms around him as tears formed in her pretty eyes and said she loved him so much as he felt her and she became aroused and asked him to make love to her. They went to the bedroom as she undressed and knelt down before Roger, looking up at him and said please master. He undressed and pulled her up before they climbed into bed together and she pleaded with him to be rough with her and talk to her in a degrading manner. Roger did as he spanked her with his hand and also slapped her, she seemed very satisfied with his treatment of her when he finished, taking her every way imaginable. They were exhausted as they lay together holding one another as she thanked him as she laid her head on his chest as he caressed her soft smooth body. After a short nap they went and took a long warm shower together as they had even more sex. Finally they finished, dried one another off and crawled back in bed and went to sleep.

Roger described to Susan the events of the previous day, and Susan said she wasn't surprised, it was just in her and the way she is. Soon they were all together upstairs as the children joined them. The years were passing as Sue Anna was now nine and Robert Walter was eight, they sat with their mom, dad and aunt for a little while like they did almost every day but were now more involved with their own adventures as they grew more aware of the world around them as children everywhere do. But today grandma and grandpa were taking them to the zoo today as they kissed them all goodbye, before running downstairs to get ready as their nanny now prepared them to leave. After the children left the three of them went downstairs for dinner and Susan suggested they go to a movie she wanted to see, they all thought that was a grand idea and after they had eaten prepared to dress as Roger called for their driver and Susan and Peggy decided on what they would wear. It was an adventure story and soon were on their way. Several hours later after they returned and undressed and relaxed as the children were back and sleeping soundly, they prepared to have a night cap before turning in; it's when Peggy said she felt funny. Roger looked at her and asked what did she meant, and said she felt really sick. He and Susan look at her closely, as Peggy started turning pale very quickly, Susan jumped up and said I think we need to call an ambulance. Peggy had never really been sick except for a cold once or twice before. Roger called 911 as Susan went and dressed hurriedly, as

Roger held her hand and told her she would be all right, when Susan returned he then went and dressed and by the time he finished the para medics had arrived. They took her vitals and said they didn't know what was happening to her as they quickly wheeled her to the elevator. Roger went with her in the ambulance, as Susan called for a driver and they quickly followed the ambulance to the hospital. After reaching the hospital, Peggy was wheeled into the emergency room where her vital signs were checked again and blood samples quickly taken. Roger told them what she had eaten last as nurses took more blood samples. Susan arrived shortly and while they looked at Peggy she opened her eyes and smiled at the two of them as Roger held her hand and bent down and Peggy said she loved him so very much and was glad he was here with her as Susan held her other hand, he kissed her forehead and said she would be all right, she turned and looked at Susan and then said, I love you sister, goodbye, Peggy then closed her pretty eyes. Then all the monitors went off as Peggy stopped breathing and a team of doctors and nurses quickly rushed in the room, checking her vital signs and trying to resuscitate her, as they placed the defibrillator on her chest, after several long minutes and several vain attempts with no response what so ever, Peggy Thomas White was pronounced dead at 11:37pm.

Roger and Susan held one another and just cried. It all happened so very suddenly, it appeared she passed away from sudden death syndrome. Susan cried like never before as Roger fought to maintain his complete composure. A doctor and nurse said they wouldn't know until the blood test came back, as they were led to a nearby waiting room as Peggy's mother and father soon arrived and shortly after Roger and Susan's parents. The emergency room doctor informed they wouldn't know for sure until all the test came back. They were preparing to leave when a doctor stopped and informed them that the cause of death had been from an opportunistic pathogen. Everyone left and returned home and Roger decided he would make the necessary arrangements the following day. It was after midnight when he and Susan returned back home. Roger and Susan decided he should call Peggy's parents and theirs in the morning and inform them he would be making the funeral arrangements. The following day after informing both families that he would take care of the funeral arrangements Roger returned to the hospital to get as many answers as possible into what had taken Peggy's young vibrant life and was soon accompanied by his father and Peggy's. A hospital administrator led the three prominent family members to a small conference room and soon the attending physician and a laboratory technician presented them with a chemical analysis that had revealed that death was due to the onset of sudden acute hepatitis and a highly inflamed liver which just shut down causing her death and was complicated by a slight case of a very acute and rare pneumonia pathogen. It was determined that for some time an invasive pathogen had been thriving in her system undetected and suddenly spread very rapidly attacking her organs, the liver, spleen, and pancreas. The doctors said with some pathogens such as the one she had, she was lucky to have lived so long. The beautiful and young Peggy Sue White had departed the world at the young age of thirty six. She had a birth day coming in a few months that she had been truly looking forward to. The doctors believed she had contacted the illness when she had been kidnapped and kept in very unsanitary conditions where the air was stagnant since the pathogens had to be airborne to have been as devastating as they were. They said what had ended her life had been seen in some prisoners of war who had consumed contaminated rice, or been held in extremely unsanitary conditions for prolonged periods of time, but it wasn't unusual to have the sudden affects that she suffered. The three men thanked the hospital as they departed and each returning to their respective homes.

The funeral was a simple and very somber affair, and was held in the same church where Peggy and Roger were married, as both families' grieved. Flags were flown at half mask in front of the ROWE headquarters building and also at the White Company building as well as ceremonial purple and black bunting had been hung at both locations. The funeral procession passed between the ROWE and White buildings and paused for a long minute on their way to the cemetery where Peggy was to be buried in a family plot with the other esteemed members of the White family. The children cried some but seemed to take the passing of their mother in stride; they were surrounded by a very loving family and knew they were loved as Ethel Anne reassured them everything would be all right. In the following weeks Roger and Susan discussed the position that Peggy held at ROWE, and said she would take on the title of CFO and CEO since the increasing and very capable staff really handled all of the day to day particulars as new management positions were created to fill the void Peggy left. The operations at ROWE continued to run smoothly and Susan visited the food distribution warehouse, not as often as Peggy, but on a fairly regular basis along with the new manager of warehouse operations and several times she was accompanied by Roger. After almost a year and a half had passed after Peggy's sudden departure and having long discussions amongst themselves. Roger and Susan finally decided to marry. They were more than satisfied with one another and had never been involved with anyone else with the exception of Peggy.

They announced to the family their intentions and Roger Sr. and Ethel Anne kind of suspected that they now would. Roger Sr. and Anne gave them their warmest blessings as they arraigned for a very simple ceremony at the church with only the immediate family and a few very close friends in attendance, and a small reception was held afterwards at home. Roger and Susan flew by private jet to Hawaii for two weeks of fun and enjoyed one another as always. On the way back he told Susan about his plans to build in Peggy's name, a housing complex in the neighborhood where she was held captive and believed that had been the beginning of her demise as he later found out after his visit to the hospital the following day with her father and his as he explained it was when she contacted the infection that had gone undetected for so long. After returning home and then returning to work. Roger assigned a team to survey the entire area where the Wine house stood, and begin acquiring the necessary adjacent properties and had several architects present him with their recommendations for his project. It was twelve weeks later when three architects presented the plans for the Peggy White gardens complex. It had been determined by only one of the three that the neighborhood was in dire need of housing for senior citizens and some who were close to becoming homeless. Roger and Susan looked at the three presentations, giving each their full and undivided attention. For them it would represent the greatest gift they could give to the one they loved and cherished so very much. The first concept was low budget, average at best and poorly designed, and also poorly presented. The second was more in line with the concept Roger had in mind, but required many more acres of land to be acquired, but consisted of several eight story buildings and several low rise building with a park like setting in the middle that was accessible from any direction. The third was eight four story buildings with easy access and large green spaces, and used the existing street grid with the streets widened and ample parking with a strip mall bordering the main development. After all the presentation and models were laid out on the large conference table Roger and Susan studied both and decided the second and third architects should work together and present a joint plan and both were contacted and a meeting was arraigned with both in attendance as he described what he liked about both as he asked them to work together and come up with a final plan. Two months later both reappeared and presented a new joint concept. It virtually meant a total re-development of the original settlement that was now part of the city. It now covered close to five hundred acres and included a new concept in the design of the shopping areas. The entire area was surrounded by homes and apartments, the streets were wide and had pedestrian over passes with all the utilities placed underground. There were homes and apartments for seniors and new families with young children and a grammar, middle and high schools would be built and all would be in walking distance with pedestrian overpasses. They both said it was totally green and energy efficient, and would be world class in design, except they placed the cost at close to six hundred million dollars to develop from start to finish. He and Susan looked at it and said they would let them know in the next few days. Roger turned to Susan and said he loved it, and would be their memorial to Peggy, a living memorial and said she would approve. Two days later when the two architects returned they found their plans had been approved and construction would begin as soon as all the land had been acquired.

It took eighteen months to acquire all the land, as construction and demolition were occurring at the same time. It took six years before the dedication and a memorial stone was placed in the center of the park and an oak tree planted that was part of the development where the new recreational center that bore the name of Peggy Sue Thomas White neighborhood center that also include a library stood. All of the members of both the White and Thomas families were in attendance, along with the mayor and other prominent government officials from the city and state in attendance. Sarah Anne, now fifteen and Robert Roger, fourteen were in attendance. Ethel Anna and Roger Sr. along with Peggy's parents Robert and Sarah Thomas all stood weeping as Roger dedicated the entire new community in her name. Roger and Susan hugged with tears in their eyes as they now toured the beautiful and modern complex. When they returned home and were sitting and having a drink the children came and hugged them both. Roger with teary eyes kissed them both and sent them on their way. Susan whispered in his ear, she had something to tell him as he looked at her. He asked her what it could be. She said she was pregnant. Roger cried like a baby as they hugged one another.

Nine months later, Peggy Susan White was born at 10 am on a Sunday morning weighing in at six pound and three ounces as the happy parents looked on. She was a healthy baby and had the look of love in her beautiful eyes as she looked up at Roger and smiled, as tears came to his eyes as he kissed Susan. It was the happiest day Roger and Susan had experienced together in a very, very long time.

The End, For Now!